Song Dogs

Song Dogs

Betty Wilson

COTEAU BOOKS
WWW.COTEAUBOOKS.COM

Edited by David Carpenter.
Cover image by Getty One.
Cover and book design by Duncan Campbell.
Illustrations by James S. McLean.
Printed and bound in Canada by Marc Veilleux Imprimeur.

National Library of Canada Cataloguing in Publication Data

Wilson, Betty, 1923-
Song dogs / Betty Wilson.

ISBN 1-55050-216-6

1. Coyotes–Juvenile fiction. I. Title.
PS8595.I58S66 2002   JC813'.54   C2002-911262-I
PZ7.W69SO 2002

10 9 8 7 6 5 4 3 2 1

401-2206 Dewdney Ave.
Regina, Saskatchewan
Canada   S4R 1H3

AVAILABLE IN CANADA & THE US FROM
Fitzhenry & Whiteside
195 Allstate Parkway
Markham, ON, Canada, L3R 4T8

The publisher gratefully acknowledges the financial assistance of the Saskatchewan Arts Board, the Canada Council for the Arts, the Government of Canada through the Book Publishing Industry Development Program (BPIDP), and the City of Regina Arts Commission, for its publishing program.

For Donald

Chapter One

The coyote pup was hiding in long grass and willow scrub that afternoon waiting for the cover of twilight, the time when it would be safe for him to start hunting. His colouring, different from the dusty tan of his litter mates, was a silvery grey tipped with darker guard hairs. So was his tail, excepting for its silver tip. At birth he had been the largest of the litter. By five weeks he was top dog. Now he was a handsome fellow, fully grown in size if not in wisdom.

Nothing moving within the range of his senses escaped him. He was watching a wedge of Canada geese pass overhead when he heard the distant wail of a train's whistle.

That brought him to his feet, sneezing with excitement. Then a dung beetle blundered out of the grass.

Silvertip started a game, laying one paw on the beetle to stop its progress, releasing it, then following it again. The beetle escaped into the crevice between two rocks. The pup was trying to dig it out when cattle appeared at the rim of the coulee with a cowboy lazing along behind them.

Remembering his mother's alarm whenever humans appeared, Silvertip huffed, bellied to the edge of the grass, held himself motionless, and tasted the breeze. His keen nose caught the odour of cow, of saddle leather, and the dangerous whiff of man, even at this distance. When the cowboy and his charges disappeared over the far rim of the coulee, the pup began leaping into the air, snatching at beards of rye grass to relieve his jittery nerves.

By the time the first stars appeared, the cowboy was forgotten. Now was the ideal hunting time, frosty and still, and the pup was hungry. His eyes adjusted perfectly to the dim light. For patient minutes he stood, one foreleg raised, body gathered, neck thrust forward, ears pricked and head turning slightly as he assessed the positions of voles scuttling along beneath the tangled grass.

When he had one pinpointed, he sprang, jack-knifed

and landed, his gathered feet stunning his victim. One snap of his jaws, three gulps, and the mouse was gone. Hunger over the past two weeks had sharpened his skills, and, since he now had his full set of second teeth, he was becoming an efficient hunter.

A humpbacked old moon was creeping above the horizon before Silvertip was satisfied. He trotted back to the spring close to the den in the bank where he had been born, drank his fill, then climbed to the rim of the coulee. The wide, inviting distances lured him, but he knew his parents would come to him. He went back to his place in the willow scrub and waited.

When the pups were six months old, the coyote family

had broken up. Now the four pups were scattered along the coulee, foraging for whatever scant pickings they could find. Instinct drove them to avoid each other. A territory can supply only so many voles, even in a good year, and this year the jackrabbit and vole population had crashed. Although the pups were learning to hunt for themselves, they still looked forward to the time when their parents visited them, each in turn, in the hour before dawn.

When Silvertip heard their high-pitched, quavering cries he began caterwauling as though he was starving, and bounded out to greet them, ears back and tail whipping. They sniffed him over while he wiggled and whined and licked their muzzles, begging them to regurgitate. While he was choking down the partially digested meat that they supplied, the parents trotted away, heading for another pup who was calling in an urgent wail from somewhere farther down the coulee.

Silvertip bounded after them. His mother rounded on him, mouth gaping, teeth gleaming. Silvertip skidded to a stop, but when his mother turned to trot after her mate, he followed again. This time, when she turned on him, she dropped her head menacingly.

Tail pumping apologies, Silvertip crawled toward her. She sprang at him, nipped him, bowled him over, and nipped him again. He fled into the willow scrub, lay nursing his sorrow, watched her disappear, then climbed to the rim of the coulee and headed north.

During the second night of his wandering, he crossed old Eli Thorne's sheep range. When he came upon the camp wagon and the drowsing herd, he quartered downwind, drinking in its odours. As always, he was hungry; he sensed that sheep would be easy prey, but his parents had never killed them.

Like most coyotes, voles were their staple diet, augmented occasionally by gophers, jackrabbits, and carrion. Besides, there was a strong human scent emanating from the camp wagon. Scary. Silvertip skirted the sheep and went on his way.

Dawn found him digging for grubs in a red ant hill beside the trail that wandered down to Thorne's ranch buildings on the flats of the South Saskatchewan River. The pup was so intent on stuffing his belly that he didn't hear the pickup until it was bumping across a Texas gate five hundred yards metres behind him.

Here was something new. Exactly what, he wasn't sure, but it intrigued him. He gawked at it, unaware that young Jake Thorne inside the pickup was gawking at him.

When Jake sprang from the truck, waving his arms and yelling, Silvertip fled. At the crest of a knoll, haloed by the rising sun, he paused to glance back, then he dropped over the hill and was gone.

Man! Wouldn't hunting coyotes be a blast? Jake leaned on the door of the pickup, staring toward the place where Silvertip had disappeared. *Why don't I hang around Alberta a while? Grandpa said he could use another hand.*

That afternoon Jake was helping Eli repair a fence, when he spotted Silvertip sniffing at a rusty oil drum over on the neighbour's land.

"Hey, Grandpa," he said, "there's that pup I saw this morning."

"Uh-huh." Eli opened the truck door, took a rifle from its sling, and slipped a bullet into the chamber.

"Lemme have a go at him. Lemme –"

"Nah. Ain't gonna shoot him. Just scare the daylights outa him and send him on his way."

The old man rested the gun on top of a fence post, sighted, and pulled the trigger. The gas barrel rang like a gong and the pup fell over himself before he fled.

Eli grinned. "That young fella's gonna get the daylights scared out of him again before morning. The old folks that

den on Dunc Ferguson's cattle operation sent their pups packing. Old Dunc never got around to getting his last hay crop off, and there's voles hiding in the grass. Figures the pair are gonna stay in his hayfield this winter. They maybe ain't gonna be too thrilled to have company."

"Dunc knows coyotes are denning on his land and he don't do anything about it?"

Eli chuckled. "Ahh. Likes to hear 'em sing. Like me." Then, sobering, "If it wasn't for the coyotes, there'd be years when the range would be crawlin' with jackrabbits and gophers and them meadow voles that make a stinkin' mess of a guy's feed stacks. Government's finally got that through *their* heads. Of course, on a cattle operation, a guy's gotta watch the coyotes at calvin' time. Otherwise, it's best not to bother 'em. Not unless one gets to thieving chickens or somethin'."

"But you're a sheep man. I thought all sheep men hated coyotes."

"Most do. Most kill a coyote whenever they get the chance. I would too if I didn't have a good herder. Old Dave's been with me since we come back from the war in '45. Honest-to-gawd old fashioned sheep herders like him are scarce as prairie chickens these days. Oh, I pay him top dollar, but there's no way I could pay him what he's *worth.*"

He chuckled. "Claims he herds the coyotes and leaves the sheep alone, and gawd knows, there's plenty of coyotes to herd. Funny thing, y'know," he added, a hint of wonder in his voice, "the coyote's been shot and poisoned and trapped ever since the country opened up, but they're holdin' their own just great.

"The thing about a coyote, though, he never makes the same mistake twice, and what he learns, he somehow knows how to pass on. They can tell each other stuff like, 'Make yourself scarce. There's a guy headed your way packing a loaded gun.' Or, 'I found something worth eating, Honey. Come and get it.' Or, 'Yippee! Tomorrow it's gonna warm up.'

"Then there's that singin' they start just about sunset. Ma, Pa, the pups, whoever. Hollering, just for the heck of it, seems like."

Silvertip had seen the humans over by the fence, but they were too far away for him to be concerned. He was more interested in the rusty oil drum. His nose warned him that this was the scent outpost of other coyotes. He was examining it with great interest when Eli's bullet smacked the barrel and rolled it a quarter-turn.

After Silvertip regained his feet, he didn't stop running until he dived into the long grass in Ferguson's hay field. He lay there, trembling and panting. All around him he could smell the recent presence of strange coyotes. He knew he should leave the field, but he could hear voles in the long grass and he was hungry. As soon as his heartbeat subsided, he began stalking them.

Greyghost and Tawny, the pair that had been denning on the cattle ranch, had been lying at the head of a draw, soaking up sun that afternoon, their responsibilities ended since their pups had dispersed. As the sun slipped toward the horizon, Greyghost rose, senses testing the surrounding prairie and the river valley below. He was a handsome animal, weighing almost fifteen kilograms and standing forty-eight centimetres at the shoulder.

Tawny, the smaller of the two, conducted her own survey. Satisfied that nothing was amiss, she bounded back to

Greyghost. As always after any parting, she wiggled before him in a belly-to-earth puppy scrunch, rose, licked his muzzle, then tapped him on the nose with her forefoot.

He accepted her homage with lordly dignity, sniffed her nose, then her hindquarters, dropped to his haunches and lifted his nose in a long sonorous wail. Tawny joined him. For a minute or two they yipped and barked and wailed in a wild duet before Greyghost stiff-shanked over to one outpost of his territory, a pile of bleached and scattered horse bones, peed over them from many angles, then raked a dusting of sand and grass over them.

Tawny was hungry. She started down the bank, headed for the hayfield. Every few steps she stopped, making sure Greyghost was following.

He took his time; he had serious duties to perform. He was examining a boulder, another of his outposts, when Eli's rifle cracked. The pair huffed with alarm, then, silent as fog, made for a saskatoon thicket in the folds of a river draw. They were a worldly-wise pair who had survived their fourth summer, where only one coyote in five lives to see its second.

They waited until deep twilight before they emerged from the thicket, climbed the bank, and stared off in the direction from which they had heard the shot. Their eyes were designed to allow them to see perfectly in fading light, but they saw nothing suspicious. Far off, in the hills, they heard the old sheep herder playing his bagpipes, a familiar sound. And a mile beyond, they heard young Jake Thorne open the pickup door to get a newspaper for his grandfather. When the house door clicked after he'd gone back inside, the coyotes headed for the hayfield, taking their time, since Greyghost insisted on stopping to piddle on each of his remaining outposts, his way of marking them as his own.

Before they reached the oil drum, they knew something was amiss. The force of Eli's bullet had rolled it a quarter-turn, more than enough to make any wily coyote suspicious. Neither would go near it. Tawny, quartering back and forth, picked up Silvertip's scent.

He was playing a game of flip-and-catch with the body of his latest victim when Greyghost and Tawny barrelled down on him. By the time he saw them, it was too late to run. Greyghost bowled him over, straddled him, and snarled dire threats while Silvertip cowered against the earth, belly and throat exposed, complete surrender his only defence.

Greyghost backed off, stalked away, and peed over a mouldy bale of hay.

As Silvertip eased onto his belly and began slinking toward the edge of the field, Tawny rushed him. He whirled to face her, but not before her teeth had torn a mouthful of hair out of his haunch. He yelped. Greyghost bowled him over again.

That time, as soon as he was allowed to rise, he tore across the field with Greyghost after him. Greyghost, finally judging the trespasser to have been suitably impressed, gave up the chase, watched Silvertip out of sight and returned to his mate.

Silvertip, clear of their range, heard the two howl triumph to each other. He piddled over a sage brush, his way of thumbing his nose at them, and went on his way.

Chapter Two

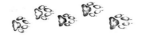

*D*awn found the pup in the tailings of an old strip mine, its banks now covered with clover and pasture sage. He had snaffled a few voles and some late sleepy grasshoppers, but he was still hungry. He scared up a covey of Hungarian partridges. They whetted his appetite for bigger game. When he sniffed into gophers' burrows, he smelled them, already hibernated and sleeping far below. Hopeless. Then he came upon the fresh moundings of a pocket gopher; its burrow passed only inches below the ground.

He dug the plug out of its tunnel; here was hopeful quarry. He began to dig, tongue lolling and yellow-green eyes glassy with desire. He found the creature trapped at

the end of a tunnel, grabbed it by its hindquarters, and yanked it out. The gopher whipped around and set its four long incisors in Silvertip's lip. He yelped and let go, but the gopher hung on. Silvertip shook his head and clawed at the beast.

When he finally shook the gopher loose, it began crawling towards its burrow. Silvertip pounced, crushed the life out of it, demolished it, then skidded his face along the ground, grunting from the pain of his bitten lip.

Before the sun rose, the pup found a patch of feathery

pasture sage, not too different in colouring from his own coat, revolved in a tight circle, trampling it to his liking, and lay down. All day he alternately dozed and surveyed his surroundings with wary senses. When evening came, he drank from a brackish pool in the mine trench before climbing to the highest point of the mine's tailings to look over the prairie.

A herd of cattle, chewing cud, were flopped out on the plain. When they lumbered to their feet and started grazing, Silvertip trotted down to mingle with them. He had learned that cattles' movements startle voles into breaking cover. He dodged among them, snaffling voles from under their heels, until the old boss cow headed for water in the mine trench. When the others strung out behind her, Silvertip left them. The instinct to move on was strong in him again.

Before nightfall of the following day he had covered a fair bit of territory, but he had found no water in his wanderings. Just as it was growing dark, he came to a highway. On the far side he smelled an artesian well. Thirsty though he was, the traffic whizzing past intimidated him. He lay in a patch of buck brush until late that night. When there had been no traffic for some time, he skipped goosily across the highway and drank his fill at the well's overflow. Scarcely had he finished when he heard a jackrabbit's scream as a speeding car flattened it onto the highway. He raced back, snatched the rabbit, carried it into the buck brush, and ate it. As he was finishing the feast, he heard the bleating death-cry of another rabbit. He streaked toward the sound.

At dawn, his belly fairly sagging, he hid in the buck brush. Along with the sickening odour of exhaust from passing traffic, he caught the fleeting odour of humans, but he saw no humans, and the highway had yielded two fine meals. When darkness came, he trotted hopefully along beside it again. That night it yielded a dead farm cat, a rabbit, and a young skunk. Before dawn, after Silvertip had drunk at the well, he crossed into a barley field, stretched out in the sun beside a swath and dozed.

That afternoon, sullen clouds moved in from the northwest. Rain began to fall. Before long, the rain turned to snow. Silvertip, snug in his double coat, merely moved to the sheltered side of the swath, rolled himself into a comfortable ball, and let the storm blow over him.

When night came, the temperature plummeted. Stinging snow rode the wind. The highway became a treacherous ribbon of ice. Senses buffeted by the storm, Silvertip moved along beside it, looking for road-kill. For a long time his search yielded him nothing besides the stench of exhaust. Then he scared up a jackrabbit. The rabbit bounded onto the highway, where a car flattened it.

Intent on retrieving his bloody prize, Silvertip dashed out onto the highway just as a farm truck barrelled down on him from the opposite direction. The pup skidded to a stop and froze, mesmerized by the blinding headlights. When the truck was almost upon him, the brakes shrieked. The truck skidded, slewing end for end. The back bumper caught Silvertip a glancing blow, somersaulted him into the ditch, and knocked him all but senseless.

The slam of the truck's door and the sound of heavy boots floundering across the highway imbued the pup with the power of pure terror. He dragged himself out of the ditch onto rough prairie, where the human would never find him in the darkness and the blinding snow.

None of Silvertip's bones were broken, no tendons were ripped, but on a night that had turned to sudden winter, instinct warned him that he would die from shock unless he found shelter. He made his painful way back to the barley field, burrowed beneath a swath, and lay for a long time, wavering between life and death.

As he warmed, he began to shiver violently, life taking hold in him again. Except for small shifts to ease his misery, he did not stir from his nest until the following night. Hunger forced him to crawl out into the starry darkness.

He had eaten nothing for two days; his layer of baby fat was rapidly depleting in the bitter cold. Every part of him was bruised and sore; he could move only with difficulty, but as soon as he saw car lights on the highway, he hobbled away from them as fast as he could go, crossed a gravelled road, and dropped down a hill into another stubble field.

There were a few voles here, but he was so slow and stiff that after hours of patient effort, he had caught only two. At daybreak, having eaten nothing besides the two voles, a few rose hips, and what fruit he could pluck out of some pincushion cacti he had found, he hid in a dry, grass-clogged slough in the middle of the field.

He was shivering, weak from hunger, but instinctively he chose a place where the camouflage of his colouring would blend perfectly with his surroundings. Curled into a tight ball to conserve body heat, motionless, except for the twitching of his ears and the movement of his yellow-green eyes, he remained pinned to the earth, looking like nothing more than a tussock of slough grass.

Late that afternoon, he heard boots crunch across the field. A man approached and stopped very close to where the pup lay. For a moment, the man seemed to Silvertip to be staring straight into his eyes. He held his place, shrinking against the earth, blood thundering through his veins.

Suddenly, the man tensed, attention caught by something farther across the field. He shifted the gun from hand to hand, pumped a bullet into the chamber and stalked away. When Silvertip heard the rifle discharge, his heart almost exploded, but he remained pinned to the earth.

Not long after, his nose caught the tantalizing whiff of meat. When he summoned the courage to peep out of the grass, he saw the man sling a coyote's hide over his shoulder and walk away.

Silvertip could scarcely contain himself until dark, but when he approached the carcass, it was befouled with the stench of man. He circled it, made feints toward it, approached it, and sprang back a dozen times before his need overcame his fear. Then he tore out great chunks of meat and gulped them down without even chewing. With his belly sagging, he curled up close by and waited until the meat was partly digested, then gorged again.

Dawn drove him back to the slough. All day he watched magpies squabble over the carcass and suppressed the desire to drive them off. At nightfall he fed again. When he had finished, only scattered bones remained.

His body was healing. A full belly insulated him against the cold, he could move without much pain, and a gentle chinook was beginning to melt the snow.

That night at dusk he mingled with a herd of range cattle. He was swallowing a vole when he heard the high-pitched "Wow-oo-wow" greeting of a strange coyote. He stood on his hind legs, head swivelling, searching for the stranger. The young female called a second time before he saw her, a shy, shadow-grey little creature.

Silvertip was entranced. A dozen times he dashed toward her. A dozen times she scampered away. When he stopped chasing her, she turned to look at him, but every time he tried to approach she skittered away. Finally, he turned away himself, pretending indifference while he sniffed at a stone. She began circling him.

He dropped into a play-inviting crouch, forelegs flattened to the earth, rump in the air, and tail waving. Shadow approached tentatively, wearing a half-submissive grin. Silvertip examined her, while she coyly averted her face, tail plastered to her rump. When he sniffed at her hindquarters, she snapped at him and sprang away.

They stood at a distance, carefully looking past each other.

Then Shadow herself fell into a play-inviting crouch. Silvertip approached cautiously. They sniffed, nose to nose. She wagged the merest tip of her tail.

He sprang away and dashed off in a giddy figure-eight race with himself before he ploughed to a stop in front of her. Shadow licked Silvertip's muzzle. He headed toward the cattle, casting an inviting glance over one shoulder. She followed.

That night they caught their fill of voles, but they were too delighted with each other to be too concerned about their bellies.

Toward morning, Shadow scared up a jackrabbit. Both pups dashed after it, but the rabbit's ten-foot leaps left them far behind. Then Silvertip remembered one of his parents' tricks. He dropped out of the race, flattened himself in the sage, and waited. Jackrabbits, for all their speed, tend to circle back over exactly the same ground.

When the rabbit bounded past a second time, Shadow

in hot pursuit, Silvertip sprang from cover. The rabbit barely had time to squeal before Silvertip's teeth dispatched it. After the pups had fed, they rubbed their faces and chins in the grass to clean themselves, then raised their noses and sang to the stars.

Chapter Three

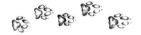

*I*n two days the chinook had melted the snow. Soon none remained, except that which clung to north-sloping fields and the shady side of rocks. The days became lazy and sun-filled, the nights frosty, brilliant with stars and the ghostly northern lights: Indian summer.

Instinct drove the pups to fatten themselves against the lean days of the coming winter. Everything huntable they hunted; everything edible they ate. They spent hours delicately picking the tart fruit from pincushion cacti. Down in the river draws, they licked up shrivelled saskatoons and chokecherries from the ground and plucked wild currants and gooseberries from the low bushes. They destroyed red ant hills, tearing them apart and eating the grubs.

Jackrabbits became easy marks. Their coats had changed from brown to white; they stood out like beacons against the dun and silver prairie. If the pups spotted one, they had become such an efficient hunting team that they generally caught it.

But as the Indian summer stretched and stretched, voles became even more scarce. The pups still found enough for their needs, but it took longer and longer each day.

Often they met older coyotes, denning pairs who had mated for life. With the food supply depleted on their summer ranges, and their litters scattered, they too had become wanderers. They examined Silvertip and Shadow in brief half-hostile, half-playful encounters, then went on their way.

But the pups also met young coyotes like themselves. The males flirted with Shadow, but if they became too bold she snapped at them querulously. She had already chosen Silvertip for her life mate. He, on the other hand, was very interested in strange females.

One evening, he and Shadow were lying in a patch of buck brush, stuffed and indolent, because that afternoon they had come across a Canada goose lost to some hunter. Shadow was loathe to move, but Silvertip was looking for action. He rose to his haunches, yipped, barked, and let go with a long quavering howl, rising in pitch and intensity, his equivalent of "Hey! Anybody out there?" From far away, other coyotes answered. Among the voices, he heard one of an intriguing young female. He answered her eagerly, shook himself from head to tail to settle his dishevelled coat, and trotted toward her voice. Shadow watched for a moment, then rose and followed him.

After they found the strange female, the three played out a three-cornered ritual, sniffing each other and skittering away. Shadow, growing tired of the game, withdrew and watched Silvertip and the stranger skip flirtatiously about in the moonlight. But when the stranger licked Silvertip's muzzle and patted him on the nose, Shadow put an end to the nonsense.

She descended on Silvertip in a jealous rage, yanked a mouthful of hair out of his haunch, and nipped him. He scuttled beyond her reach, turned, looked past her, and wagged his tail at the strange female.

Enraged, Shadow turned on the female, chased her down a coulee bank, across the coulee bottom, and up its far side before she quit. The stranger was still running flat out when Shadow, still snorting indignation, trotted back to Silvertip, licked his muzzle, patted him on the nose, cavorted around him, then threw her head back and shouted her triumph.

After a moment, Silvertip joined her in a wild duet. She trotted confidently away then, Silvertip following, a suggestion of smug satisfaction in his gait.

*I*n late October, when the river froze, the two crossed to the north side. Up beyond the banks, stubble fields stretched to the horizon. Voles were more plentiful there; so were farm buildings. Human beings came and went among the buildings, and trucks clattered along the gravelled roads.

The pups avoided the buildings, never revealing their presence in daylight, but one farm intrigued them. At dusk, turkeys roosted in the poplars surrounding the yard. At dawn, before humans were stirring in the house, the turkeys flew down from the trees and wandered about the farm yard hunting for food.

One morning, a tom turkey ventured into the stubble field where Silvertip and Shadow were hiding. Shadow streaked for it and killed it before it even had time to squawk. The two dragged it into the pasture, out of sight of the farm buildings, and feasted royally.

When a man came out to drive the cows home at milking time, the pups watched him from deep in the stubble field as he kicked at turkey feathers in a patch of buck brush.

The next morning, no turkeys roosted in the poplars.

When the pups approached the buildings, Silvertip noticed a door in the hayloft standing slightly open. Yesterday, it had been closed. He would not go near the place, but Shadow, the bolder of the two, was making a foray toward the yard when she heard something move in the loft. She fled.

A rifle cracked and a bullet zipped past her shoulder. Again the rifle cracked. A clod of dirt exploded at her heels. The next bullet ticked the tip of her right ear. She rolled, regained her feet, and landed running flat out. She was two fields away, trembling under a caragana windbreak, when Silvertip found her.

The tip of her right ear, attached by only a bit of skin, hung like a ragged flap. Blood trickled down her face and onto her shoulder. Silvertip gently licked the blood away, but it was a long time before Shadow quit trembling.

As soon as darkness came, the two headed across the river again, back to the slim pickings of voles and jackrabbits.

Winter came with gentle snow drifting like feathers in the night. The pups were ecstatic. They burrowed in it, rolled in it, and chased each other in rowdy games of tag. But under its blanket, voles became even more elusive, and as the snow piled up day by day, jackrabbits snow-shoed across the drifts while Shadow and Silvertip broke through. Floundering back to firm footing on high ground used up precious energy.

Many days they caught next to nothing. Much of the time they were hungry. Both were losing weight.

Then, one day, they had a most puzzling encounter. It was high noon; the sun, low in the winter sky, was lighting the snow covered prairie with an almost blinding brilliance. Silvertip and Shadow were holed up, waiting for a time when they would be less visible before they started hunting, when they saw a young coyote approaching.

The stranger was staggering. Sometimes it fell, dragging itself back to its feet only with difficulty. Huffing their dismay, the pups watched it for some time, then curiosity getting the better of them, they went out to investigate. They challenged the stranger, but it merely staggered past as though it had not seen them. They followed, sniffing at it curiously and prodding it with their noses while it floundered away, weaving drunkenly though the snow, too sick to pay them any attention.

Puzzled, the two watched it out of sight, then, since they were up and about anyway, forgot about it and went off to hunt voles. What they did not know was that the stranger was in the early stages of distemper, one of the most deadly and most contagious of all canine diseases.

Three days later both pups felt unwell. Fits of shivering overtook them; they had no desire to hunt. They did not even have the will to investigate a herd of pronghorns that had been driven across the river by the winter storms, although these were the first pronghorns they had ever seen.

That afternoon, the full misery of distemper descended on them. Fever raged in them and violent fits of shivering overtook them. The glare of the low sun on the snow tortured their eyes. They wavered down into a river draw to find shelter, and curled up in a chokecherry thicket out of sight of enemies, and out of reach of the worst of the wind.

Fever consumed them. The prairie tipped and spun when they raised their heads, but after the second day, the fever subsided. They emerged from the draw, wobbly, body fat depleted, but with no desire for food and no will to hunt.

When the fever struck the second time, the most deadly time, the pups did not even have the will to find decent shelter. They curled up beside sage bushes out on the open plains, racked by attacks of vomiting and diarrhea, noses dripping, red-rimmed eyes scummy with pus, and bodies jerking and twitching in helpless convulsions.

After the third day the sickness abated, but the pups were too weak to leave their befouled nests. Toward the end of that short December day, when they heard rifle shots, they were too close to death even to be afraid.

Snow began to fall, gently at first, then in a blinding smother. With the coming of darkness, the pups heard the laboured breathing of a wounded pronghorn. Lost to hunters in the snow, it had staggered as far as its strength would allow, then collapsed and died not far from where the pups lay.

The smell of blood brought them wavering out to investigate. As they licked tentatively at the crimson snow around the carcass, hunger awakened. They ripped the hide, then guzzled the antelope's sweet, sagey meat, snapping half-heartedly at magpies who came to share the feast when daylight came.

For three days they fed while strength returned. They were not yet fully recovered, but fortune had spared them distemper's worst legacy; the savage disease had not permanently damaged their nervous systems.

When the pronghorn was nothing but gnawed bones, hunger forced them to start hunting again, but day after day storm followed storm, piling the prairie with snow.

The coyotes had to test their footing constantly to find drifts solid enough to support their weight.

During the cruel days grinding down to the winter solstice, they drifted onto Wally Johnson's two-bit cattle operation, while the north wind sucked heat from their skinny bodies. They searched for voles, but the sloughs where they might have found them were piled from rim to rim with snow.

Toward the middle of December, nature unleashed her full fury. Two killer blizzards struck the prairie, one on the heels of the other. Huge drifts, formed and reformed by the wind, piled on the leeward side of knolls while all life sank into itself and clung grimly to survival.

Wally Johnson, on whose lands the pups were wandering, had stockpiled a minimum of cattle feed, gambling on it being one of southern Alberta's open winters when stock can graze out on the range a good deal of the time. By December his stockpile was gone, and cattle feed was almost impossible to come by anywhere on the prairies. During the second blizzard, Johnson's cattle, driven by wind and moaning from cold, drifted down into the snow-clogged river draws seeking shelter. A half dozen mired there and died before he located feed and got it out to them.

During the same blizzard, old Eli Thorne died of a heart attack while he struggled to help Jake and the herder keep the ewes from piling up in the corral and smothering one another.

Jake was shocked. He had become quite fond of his old grandfather, but as soon as he decently could after the funeral, he packed his gear and was ready to depart. Sheep ranching was anything but romantic, he had discovered, and he had not shot a single coyote.

But the day before he was to leave, a letter arrived from his grandfather's lawyer. When Jake discovered that he had inherited the ranch, his delight was tempered when the accountant who examined the accounts said, "Well, the ranch *was* making it. Just. Trouble is, your grandfather paid that old coot of a sheep herder more than he paid himself. Cheaper to run a pack of coyote hounds, I'd think. More fun, too."

"Coyote hounds? Yeah, right on! Soon as lambing's over next spring, I'm gonna can that herder and get me a pack of hounds. And if there's anything I need to know about sheep, I'll just write to the Department of Agriculture, eh? They've probably got all kinds of stuff on killing coyotes, too."

Chapter Four

But for Shadow and Silvertip the humans' disaster provided a windfall of riches. Soon there was more carrion than they could eat. Before long, Greyghost and Tawny appeared to share in their bounty, since the heavy snowfall on Ferguson's hay field had made hunting voles there all but impossible. A couple of days later, Slim and Dusty, two-year-olds who had yet to produce their first litter, joined the other four.

Aside from minor squabbles over the hierarchy of who should feed first, the coyotes could afford the luxury of each other's company. Soon they began to operate as a loosely formed pack, dominated by Greyghost and Tawny.

One night another hard-bitten couple appeared and

attempted to attach themselves to the pack. The female, Limpy, had lost a front foot in a trap. The injury had healed; she travelled surprisingly well on three legs, but her mate was in a bad way.

A choking wire noose encircled his neck. A weird squalling sound came from his throat, and he could scarcely breathe. Three days ago, when he had been feeding at the carcass of a dead cow on another ranch, he had torn a snare loose from its moorings before it choked him to death, but in the struggle the wire had kinked back on itself. It would not slide through the loop and release. Squall could scarcely breathe, let alone swallow, and although he was starving to death, he was too suspicious to approach a carcass where other coyotes were not already feeding.

The pack, wary of his snoring breath and the weird sounds coming from his throat, would have nothing to do with him. Whenever he and Limpy tried to approach a carcass where the pack were feeding, they took off.

They were taking turns feeding on a dead cow on the far side of the range, when Limpy and her partner approached for the third time. The male was desperate. He hunched his back in an alley-cat stance, teeth gaping threats, the ridge of hair along his back standing on end, while he sneaked in beside Silvertip and tried to feed. Silvertip slashed at him.

When the stranger ducked away, the tip of the dead cow's horn hooked under the snare around his neck. Crazed with fear, he began to struggle. The pack huffed alarm at his strangled squalls and melted into the darkness, but Limpy stayed close to her mate, trotting anxiously back and forth while he gagged and choked and whimpered. At last, ignoring the agony of the wire cutting into his neck, he braced his feet and threw his weight against the snare. Slowly, the kink straightened. The wire abruptly slipped through the loop.

Squall landed head over heels in the snow, his neck cruelly cut. But he was free.

He swallowed great gulps of snow, tobogganed through it, rubbed his face and neck in it, lifted his head, croaked a time or two, then managed one triumphant squawky squall.

Limpy hobbled to him and tenderly licked his raw neck, then the two returned to the cow where the pack had been feeding.

Although Squall was starving, and he had seen coyotes

eating there only minutes before, it was a long time before he could conquer his suspicion and begin to feed himself, but after daring the first gulp, he tore at the carcass, gulping and half choking on great hunks of scarcely-chewed meat.

The pack appeared, ready to assume their feast. Squall warned them off. Not even Greyghost would challenge him. There were other carcasses where the pack could have fed. Instead, they curled up on the snow, eyeing Squall with miserable, jealous expressions, watching him stuff himself.

But in a day or two, the pack's reservations toward the strangers evaporated. Life was easy. They were all becoming fat and sassy. They could afford the energy to indulge themselves in giddy games of tag. Soon Squall and Limpy had blended into the pack.

January was bitterly cold, but day by day the sun was creeping back. Hormones were beginning to stir. In another month the females would be ready to have pups. An instinct to court baby-sitters to help take care of their unborn litters began working in Tawny and Limpy. Since

Silvertip and Shadow were too young to have pups of their own until the following season, they came in for a good deal of attention as possible baby-sitters. Limpy became chummy with Shadow while Tawny made overtures to Silvertip. Often they romped with the youngsters, or curled up in the snow close beside them to snooze.

Shadow wavered between Limpy's flattering wooings and her loyalty to Silvertip. Silvertip, on the other hand, was enthralled by Tawny's attentions. But, as the actual mating season drew nearer, he found himself in a confusing predicament. So long as Greyghost was not about, Tawny was flirtatious with him, playful. The moment Greyghost appeared, Tawny ignored him. Greyghost punished him if he so much as glanced in her direction. Not severely at first. Just enough to teach him his place.

But as the last days of January arrived, tensions mounted. Jealous skirmishes broke out among the pack, with threats and displays of teeth. Each mating pair began keeping to itself. The males became savage at any hint of intrusion, even from potential baby-sitters.

Fortunately, Wally Johnson's mind was on coyote traps, not on coyotes, the time he rode within a stone's throw of Greyghost and Tawny while they were mating. He did not see them. He had stopped to stare speculatively at a dead cow before Greyghost and Tawny could get away. As soon as they could, they bellied off through the grass, heading for old Dunc Ferguson's hay field, as fast as they could go.

Nobody needed to tell Squall and Limpy that the rider was trouble. They fled across the river ice, heading for the abandoned farm where they had denned the previous summer.

Slim and Dusty trailed them as far as the sheep ranch, where Dusty discovered an abandoned badger burrow in the river bank, a fine place to excavate a den. And with water close by, and a bellyful of puppies started, what better place to raise her first family? For a long time neither the sheepherder nor young Jake Thorne knew that they were there.

Silvertip and Shadow were left behind on Johnson's land. They had seen Wally riding across his land, too, but they knew he hadn't seen them. Besides, the chinook that had ripped over the Rockies three days before had uncovered carcasses no coyote had ever touched.

Chapter Five

A good coyote pelt was worth sixty-five dollars that year, and Wally's money situation was becoming grim. That afternoon he had dug the gunny sack with his trapping gear out of the manure pile, where it had been curing for a couple of weeks, hung it from his saddle horn, and headed for the river draws.

He considered several carcasses before he settled on one that the melting snow had only recently exposed. Before he dismounted, he put on a pair of manure-soaked gloves, fished a couple of gunny sacks, similarly treated, out of the sack that was hanging from his saddle horn, and dropped them to the ground. He stepped down onto one of the sacks, spread the other, laid a hammer, three coyote traps, and some metal stakes on top of it.

Careful not to touch the earth and contaminate it with his scent, he knelt on the other sack and scooped a depression into the snow beside the carcass. He spread the jaws of the trap, triggered it, laid a piece of cloth over the pan, then gingerly set the trap into the depression he had scooped. After he pounded the stake into the earth and attached the trap's chain to it, he covered his handiwork with snow and dusted it delicately with a twig of sage brush.

Moving from gunny sack to gunny sack, he set two more traps before he mounted his horse. Hanging from the saddle horn, he reached down, picked up his gear, backed his horse off and looked at his work. Not far from where he had set the traps he caught a flash of movement as a badger backed into its hole.

"That one could be trouble," he muttered. "Let him find a trapped coyote and sure as heck he'll eat the coyote, and there goes my pelt." He hesitated, then shrugged. "Well, too late to move traps now. Gotta take my chances."

That night Shadow and Silvertip paddled through the icy slush, poking into this draw and that, until they found the heifer that Wally had staked out. No coyote had fed there. Shadow would not go near it, but Silvertip sensed that there was an unborn calf in the dead heifer's belly. The choicest of tidbits. The fat days of the past month had dulled Silvertip's natural wariness. He inched in, sank his teeth into the flank, braced his feet, and was yanking on the hide to tear it when one hind foot touched cold steel.

The trap closed with a vicious snap, two of Silvertip's toes gripped in its teeth. Pain burst through his foot and up his leg. He tried to spring away. The trap's chain brought him crashing to the ground. He scrambled to his feet, whimpering and scrabbling at the frozen earth while he struggled to pull himself free. Useless. Exhaustion left him panting and trembling.

He attacked the trap with his teeth. Frozen steel ripped skin from his tongue and lips. Again he fought to pull free, joints cracking with the effort. The trap held. He flopped, spread-eagled on the snow, eyes glazed, terror giving way to despair. Mercifully, his foot and leg were becoming numb.

Shadow, who had fled up the draw, trotted back and forth, huffing with alarm. Now, after many false starts and backward leaps, she came to Silvertip, licked his muzzle and sniffed along the length of his body. When her nose touched the trap that held him, she leapt away. Her foot grazed another. It clanged shut. She fled. She would not go near Silvertip again.

He struggled until he was exhausted, gathered his strength, and struggled again. He did not know that his efforts had pulled the jaws of the trap down to the tip of one toe just above the nail, and to the first knuckle of the other, but now he was reaching the point of complete exhaustion. The times when he lay recovering his strength grew longer as the night grew older, and each new struggle was less determined than the last.

It was Shadow who spotted the badger standing above her at the head of the draw, head weaving, as Silvertip, in a desperate bid to free himself, had started to chew off his own toe. The badger cocked its head, listening, then waddled down the bank, all deadly business.

A badger had eaten two of Shadow's litter mates when she was three weeks old. It had taken both parents and a yearling brother to drive it off. Courage and hatred wakened in her now. She whipped past the beast, slashing at its rump. It paused, hissing. When it turned away, Shadow whipped past again. That time her teeth drew blood. The badger bumbled after her. She skipped away.

The beast turned, coarse guard hairs on end, muttering in its throat and headed for Silvertip. Again Shadow drew blood. The badger lunged at her the next time she raced past. Foot by slow foot, the two fought their way down the bank to where Silvertip was trapped.

The badger rushed him. Silvertip screamed and leapt the length of his chain, tearing off one toe and the nail of another to free himself. But now he was exhausted, slow, suffering from shock. The badger was almost upon him when Shadow sank her teeth into its back again and hung on. The two rolled over each other three times before Shadow let go. The badger swiped at her with claws that could have disembowelled her if she had not been quick enough to elude them. By that time Silvertip was safely out of range.

Shadow followed, whipping around repeatedly in case the badger should pursue, but it rolled to its feet and waddled toward the dead cow, muttering in its throat. The last the pups heard of it was its roar of rage and pain when it blundered into Wally's third trap.

The pups, badly in need of some hiding place where they could recover, found a rock overhang jutting out of the river bank where the earth was dry. Silvertip, exhausted and suffering from shock, curled up in a ball and shivered miserably until the rising sun warmed him when it found their hiding place. Then he began licking his bloody foot.

As soon as twilight came, Shadow went to hunt. Although the vole population had all but disappeared, she would not go near the cow carcasses scattered through the river draws. To hunt jackrabbits alone was a waste of energy, and no migrating birds worth hunting had yet returned to the prairies. Again and again she returned to Silvertip, having found nothing but a few dried rose hips, but he would not touch them. He burned with fever, constantly licking his foot, which had become putrid with infection.

As the weather warmed, the breeze carried tantalizing odours of decay from the carcasses rotting in the river draws, but nothing could have induced Shadow to go near them. She and Silvertip starved in the midst of plenty.

Driven by desperation, she began to hunt in broad daylight. On the open prairie, she discovered recently-awakened male gophers squabbling over breeding territory. Here was food, but she had had no experience in catching them. Last summer, they had hibernated before she was mature enough to try. As well, few coyotes are brave enough to take on a fully grown male gopher.

But now, after spotting one, she would creep along the earth, freezing the moment the gopher lifted its head from grazing, then steal forward another few feet, every sense trained on the gopher, until, when she was close enough, she would rush it in what looked like a sure catch. But the gopher never strayed far from its burrow. Time after time Shadow tumbled head over heels when one dived into its hole and eluded her.

When she finally came upon one separated from its burrow and tackled it, the gopher put up a wicked fight. She ended up with a cruelly bitten nose before she could dispatch the creature, but she immediately gobbled it down, hurried back to Silvertip and regurgitated the meat for him. He was too sick to touch it. Instead, he staggered out to eat snow that remained in the shadow of some rocks, then staggered back to his hiding place to lick his foot again.

He had been a strong, young coyote in prime condition; now he was an emaciated skeleton, his handsome coat dulled like that of a dead creature. Still, his body defences were beginning to fight. The fifth day after his injury, bits of dead tissue were still sloughing off the foot and it still oozed pus, but the infection was subsiding. Then, suddenly, he was over the hump. And starving. Hobbling on three legs, he followed Shadow out to hunt.

Although they tried for hours every day, they barely caught enough to keep them alive, and all the time the winter-killed cattle lay, tantalizingly swelling and stinking in the sun.

Then Silvertip realized that whenever Shadow ran a gopher to earth, it appeared a minute or two later to squeak mocking hysteria at them from a few metres away at the entrance of its ventilation hole. The next time Shadow holed one, Silvertip was waiting at the gopher's back door. The lean times were ending, and although Silvertip's damaged foot was still too tender to use, it was healing.

Chapter Six

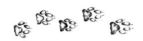

Jake Thorne was determined to fire the old sheepherder as soon as lambing was finished. The herder's wages were biting too deeply into the profits of the ranch.

Jake wrote to the Department of Agriculture for literature on predator control. He acquired the necessary tools for snaring coyotes or killing them in their dens, and stowed the equipment in his pickup. Then he heard of a pack of coyote hounds for sale. He couldn't resist. He was headed for home with the four of them under the new canopy on the back of his pickup when he spotted Silvertip and Shadow.

"Two of 'em! And on my land, too. Well, here goes."

The moment the coyotes saw the truck turn in their direction, they took off, Silvertip running on three legs.

With the truck practically within spitting distance of the coyotes, Jake hit the brakes, came to a screeching halt, tumbled out, yanked the canopy open, and yelled, "Go get 'em, boys!"

A rangy brute, part Irish wolfhound, spotted the coyotes. His long strides ate distance. The other three, bellowing for blood, streamed after him. Jake leapt into the truck and sent it careening in reckless pursuit.

The coyotes skinned under old Dunc Ferguson's fence, the hounds streaming after them with scarcely a break in stride.

Jake crowed, "No time flat they're gonna have that grey son-of-a-gun that's runnin' kinda funny. I'm not missing this." He sprang from the truck, snatched wire cutters from behind the seat, cut Dunc's fence, and sent the truck roaring through the gap in hot pursuit.

Then that "grey son-of-a-gun that was runnin' kinda funny" fled over the crest of a knoll, momentarily out of sight of the hounds, and seemingly evaporated. One second it was there, leading the hounds by a few hundred strides; the next it was gone. The hounds, coursers who hunt by sight rather than by scent, passed over the place where Silvertip had disappeared, still tearing after Shadow.

"Idiot hounds ran right over that coyote!" Jake roared.

He stopped the truck at the spot where he'd last seen Silvertip, sprang out, grabbed the rifle from its sling, and began kicking through the sage.

"But where'd he *go?*" he raged. "Where *could* he go? Unless he changed into a rattlesnake or a beetle or something.... He's sure not here."

But he was. Jake was standing only a few feet from Silvertip at that very moment.

With the hounds in close pursuit, Silvertip had had but one hope, and that a desperate one. The moment he got a knoll between himself and the hounds, he skidded into the grass, made himself one with the prairie, and lay absolutely still, his only movement the thunder of his heart quivering with every beat through the tips of his ears.

"Beats me. But I can hear the hounds bellering after that other one down in the river draws. We'll get one of 'em, anyhow."

Jake jumped back into the truck, slammed it into gear and stomped on the gas. He was tearing across Dunc's land when the front wheels of the pickup hit a deep stock trail. The truck jarred to a stop, the engine stalled, and Jake almost went through the windshield. While he gathered his wits and fingered the goose egg growing on his forehead, he looked down at the river. There he saw Shadow almost at the far side, picking her way across the rotting ice.

"Fool hounds missed that one, too," he groaned. "Well, I've had it with chasing coyotes for a while. Gonna whistle the hounds back and call it a day."

Limpy and Squall, whose puppies were almost due, had heard the hullabaloo from where they were hiding in a patch of rose briers on the far side of the river. They were scared. More than once they had escaped hounds, barely with their lives, and now only the rotting ice separated them.

When Shadow dragged herself up the bank, trembling and exhausted, the two jumped her, bowled her over, yanked out mouthfuls of hair, and threatened worse. Shadow could do nothing but offer herself in ignominious surrender, belly and throat exposed. Squall was standing over her, snarling into her face and daring her to move when Limpy shouldered him aside. She sniffed Shadow attentively as though reminding herself of something. Then she allowed Shadow to roll to her belly.

When Shadow did so, dropping her head submissively, the two sniffed nose to nose. The stiff hackles on Limpy's shoulders relaxed. She eased onto one hip and grunted a little, as though seeking comfort from her bellyful of pups before she began tenderly washing Shadow's face.

Chapter Seven

After Silvertip saw the truck limp back through the gap in the fence, he rose, trembling from exhaustion. Although he was keenly aware that he was now trespassing deep into Tawny and Greyghost's territory, he began to look for Shadow. Several times he found traces of her scent, but it was always contaminated with the frightening odour of hounds.

After dark he gave up and was heading back toward neutral ground when he saw the truck return and stop at Dunc's fence. Its long beams shone into Silvertip's eyes. Whatever terrors a meeting with Greyghost might hold for him, they were nothing compared to his terror of that truck and its occupant. He would not go near it, even to pass.

What he did not know was that Jake Thorne had had his ears pinned back. Old Dunc Ferguson, his grandfather's very good friend and neighbour, had been waiting for Jake when he arrived home with the hounds. Dunc was blunt. "You cut my fence, Mister. You fix it."

"Absolutely, Dunc. First thing in the –"

"Now."

"But it's almost dark."

"Somethin' wrong with headlights on that truck?"

"No, but –"

"Then, get at it. Somethin' they never learned you in Toronto, I guess. In the ranchin' country, nobody messes with another man's fence. Now, get your ass in gear."

Late that night, Tawny and Greyghost discovered Silvertip hesitating at the edge of their hayfield. When they rushed him, he dropped his head, tucked his tail between his legs, revolving in a circle, his back in an alley-cat arch, hair on end, the threat of his gleaming teeth denied by the helpless piddle leaking onto the frozen grass. At Tawny's approach, he stopped his gyrations and wagged the merest tip of his tail. Greyghost knocked him flat.

Silvertip grovelled, belly exposed, legs waving. Greyghost backed off, peed over a sage bush, cast Silvertip a contemptuous glance, raked dirt over him and stalked away with the lordly air of one who has had the ultimate say. As Silvertip rolled to his belly, Tawny approached, playfully laying one paw on his back. He rose to face her, tail plastered to his butt, the tip wagging. She dropped into a play-inviting crouch, rising to face him when he approached. They circled. He sniffed at her hindquarters. She slashed at him. He yelped and sprang away. She turned to follow Greyghost.

When Silvertip gathered his courage and loped after them, the pair, like a couple of mischievous children, had concealed themselves behind a pile of rock to wait for him. At his approach, they sprang from cover to bar his path. He skidded to a stop and assumed his alley-cat hunch. After they had examined him again, Silvertip stopped circling and dared a glance at Tawny from the corner of his eye, dropped his head humbly, and pulled his mouth into a suitably submissive grin.

Nose to earth and head weaving, she moved away from him, heading into the wind. When she found a fresh cow flap, she dropped a shoulder and rolled through it, then rose, suitably perfumed, casting Silvertip an inviting glance over one shoulder. Then she trotted after Greyghost, who was headed for an enormous granite boulder that some glacier, ages ago, had dropped and forgotten in what was now old Dunc Ferguson's pasture.

Long before humans had walked this land, Greyghost's kind had sung from this eminence. When the three climbed to its top now, Greyghost threw back his head and started to sing. The others joined him, full voice.

Suddenly the night was alive with coyote song, echoing with ventriloquist's magic, from family to family, back and forth across the river valley. Warnings, greetings, threats and a little hollering just for the heck of it. Slim and Dusty challenged from the sheep ranch, Limpy and Squall from across the river.

Among their voices, Silvertip recognized another – Shadow's. But now her voice held the challenge of her allegiance to Limpy and Squall. Silvertip threw his own voice back across the distance, defiantly proclaiming *his* allegiance to Tawny and Greyghost.

When the yip-howl session ended, Tawny, followed by her entourage, headed for her favourite den. She was about to enter and tidy it up when the river ice heaved, boomed like twenty cannons, and split from shore to shore. Tawny exploded out of the den. All three had run halfway across

Dunc's pasture before they dared to stop and look back. Tawny would never go near that particular den site again so long as she lived.

She investigated several other possible denning sites before she came upon a badger's excavation halfway up the bank in a secluded draw. Ideal. The river was close by, the site was concealed in wild currant and chokecherry bushes, no animal trails passed near it, and there was no hint that humans ever visited the place.

The badger had gone to considerable effort to satisfy his taste for hibernating gophers. His tunnel extended several feet back into the bank; Tawny's work was already half done. She had merely to enlarge the tunnel and, at the far end, scoop out a den just big enough so that she could stand up inside and turn around. As she dug herself out of sight, Greyghost followed, raking her diggings back through the passage and out through the tunnel's mouth.

Silvertip took no part in the operation. He acted as lookout and nosed about the bank, searching for anything that he might eat.

Dawn was approaching before Tawny was satisfied with her handiwork. She came back along the tunnel, facing Greyghost, who was raking out the last of her diggings, and backed him outside. The two greeted as though congratulating each other on a night's work well done, rolled in the grass, shook their dishevelled coats, headed for the river, and drank at the water's edge.

The stars were dimming when they reached the hayfield whose vole population was nicely recovering from the previous summer's dearth. Dawn was only just breaking before they had satisfied their hunger.

As the birth of the puppies approached, they became most secretive. The moment daylight came, they holed up. Old Dunc had not caught a glimpse of them for a month. If he had not heard them howling sometimes after dark, he would not have known they were there.

The day after Silvertip joined them, the pair chose a patch of buck brush on the open plain for their hiding place. The brush was scant enough for them to see in all directions; at the same time, it hid them from view and offered some protection from the chinook which would punish the prairie after the sun rose.

And punish it did. Russian thistles rolled and skipped before the wind, ploughed land rose in dusty clouds, cattle, inflamed eyes streaming tears, sought shelter in the draws, and horses turned rumps to the chinook, manes and tails tangling and scattering before the wind. But the coyotes rolled into tight balls and flattened to the earth while the rushing sea of air howled and moaned above them. Toward evening, when the wind died, they heard a flock of squabbling magpies. That meant carrion. At dark they went to investigate.

One of Dunc's cows had given birth to a malformed calf and wandered away. The ranch collie was worrying the carcass now. The collie held no terror for the coyotes. When he had been young and foolish, Tawny, out of pure mischief, had once lured him out into the pasture where she and Greyghost gave him a wicked beating. The moment he saw the coyotes he streaked for home.

Although they had seen the collie feeding on the calf, the coyotes did not approach it at once. They quartered back and forth, downwind, senses straining. Satisfied that there was no danger, Greyghost at last moved in. Tawny joined him and the two began to feed. Whenever Tawny wanted some choice tidbit for herself, she slammed Greyghost with her hip. He always gave way with an expression of hurt surprise. With the birth of their puppies imminent, he indulged her slightest whim.

Silvertip did not presume to approach while the pair

fed, but even so, they looked up at him from time to time and warned him off. After they had eaten the best meat, they began cleaning themselves in the grass, huffing with belly-full satisfaction while Silvertip apologized his way past them. He had touched no carrion since he'd lost his toes in the trap, but here Tawny and Greyghost had come to no harm. When he began feeding, he gulped great mouthfuls, choked, regurgitated, and ate the meat again.

When he could hold no more, he cleaned himself, then hurried to catch up to Tawny and Greyghost who were standing shoulder to shoulder, dodging playful feints of each other's teeth. Tawny rolled over while Greyghost, uttering affectionate threats, chewed behind one of her ears. With a lightning flirt, she was on her feet, nipped at his foreleg, whipped away, turned to plough to a stop in front of him, tapped him smartly on the nose and licked his muzzle.

Silvertip, longing to join in the fun, galloped back and forth, stopping to drop into play-inviting crouches, but the pair ignored him. Finally, they threw back their heads and began to sing. That, at least, Silvertip could do. He joined in, tentatively at first, then with growing confidence; he had the makings of a very fine singer.

Although he spent his days lazing in some patch of buck brush or rose briers with Tawny and Greyghost, he put his nights to good use. His skinny carcass was filling out, his foot had healed, and he was regaining his confidence, but he always found urgent business to attend to elsewhere whenever Greyghost stopped to look directly at him. Greyghost barely tolerated him; he never quite forgave Silvertip for having been so chummy with Tawny the previous winter.

Silvertip got his kicks elsewhere. He followed an old badger, tormenting him unmercifully. While the beast dug for gophers, Silvertip waited at the gopher's ventilation hole, snatching the prey before the badger had a hope of getting to it. He cleaned up on mallards' nests, too, not to mention those of lark buntings and meadowlarks, and his contributions to the nightly singsongs were becoming outstanding.

Often, during the howling rituals, Silvertip picked up Shadow's voice along with those of Limpy and Squall. But for the time being, her voice, like his own, proclaimed loyalty to the pair that had adopted them.

Old Dunc stopped to listen to the coyotes one night after he'd run the cows that were about to calve into the

corral. "Hear them coyotes?" he asked his wife as he entered the house. "Gonna be a change in the weather, sounds like."

"About time that chinook blew itself out. Gets me down in the springtime when it starts blowing and don't know when to quit."

The chinook did indeed blow itself out. Day after day a warm sun shone from a cloudless sky and spring came in a sweet, glorious rush. The air was filled with the wings of birds: ducks, their stubby wings pumping frantically, and great spearheads of Canada geese. Day and night they passed, graceful terns, and tiny song birds twittering in starlight.

The prairie wakened from its winter sleep. Sunlight

coaxed new grass through the dusty clumps of prairie wool, gummy buds swelled on the Balm o' Gileads in the river valley, and the prickly pear cacti stiffened their spines as their panicles swelled. The prairies were ablaze with golden buffalo beans, and even the sage greened to a less sullen shade of grey.

Young calves bucked and played in Dunc's pastures, and lambing was in full swing on Jake Thorne's sheep ranch.

There had been another birth on the sheep ranch too. A very secret one. Slim and Dusty had eight fuzzy babies hidden in a den in a river draw, a very large litter indeed.

Chapter Eight

Slim was having it rough. The demands of eight puppies on Dusty's milk were leaching her very bones. She was always ravenous. Slim worked overtime trying to catch enough game to keep her fed, but nothing he caught was enough, and he had no babysitter to lighten his load.

The lambs began to look very tempting. They would be easy prey, but during the daytime, there was always a man with a collie near the flock. When the sheep moved, the man followed, and took up his station from the top of another knoll.

For several nights, while the flock was bedded close beside the buildings, Slim crept in close, quivering with temptation as he stared at the lambs, but a man with a lantern that cast great, scissoring, black shadows, often moved around the outer periphery of the flock looking for any ewe that might be in trouble birthing a lamb, or for new births where the mother and her baby needed to be put in the lambing shed.

Slim smelled hounds too, but he had no experience with them; he didn't know how dangerous they were. It was the man who scared the stuffing out of him. Whenever he appeared, Slim lost his nerve and took to the prairies again.

Often, after hours of hunting, he returned to Dusty with only a few voles and some beetles in his belly. After he had regurgitated for her, he was hungry himself.

But late one night he had a rare bit of luck. He came upon a wounded pronghorn. As he circled the pronghorn, assessing his chances, the creature turned to face him, hair ridging along its neck and shoulders. Although it had lost a great deal of blood, it was full of fight. When Slim approached, it lowered its head and charged him. He scampered out of its way. A pronghorn's sharp hooves are deadly weapons. But Slim knew the creature would die; he had only to wait.

At dawn, he approached the pronghorn again.

Weakened by shock and loss of blood, it staggered away a few steps, then collapsed in a tangle of legs. In a flash, Slim was at its throat. Before it was dead, he was feeding.

The pronghorn, shared with magpies, some gophers, an old boar badger, and a number of crows, lasted Slim and Dusty for four days; then they were back to lean pickings. The lambs looked more and more tempting. Still, Slim might never have found the courage to steal one if the old sheepherder had not stepped on a rusty nail and got such a bad infection that he had to be hospitalized for a couple of days. Jake, who took over as night man, was neither so dedicated as the herder nor so wise.

Before midnight that first night he was asking himself, "Why don't I stretch out on that bale of straw there for ten minutes before I make another circle of the flock?" The "just ten minutes" became more like an hour.

Since no man had appeared for a long time, Slim, who was watching from out in the sage, began creeping closer and closer to the drowsing flock. A lamb at the periphery of the band rose, stretched, bleated, and began stumbling among the ewes, searching for its dam. The temptation was too much.

Slim rose to a crouch, his total concentration on the

lamb. A scuttling rush, one crunch of his jaws on the lamb's head, and it was dead.

Instant pandemonium. Ewes sprang to their feet. Lambs bleated and blundered through the flock looking for dams. Jake burst out of the lambing shed, surmised what had happened, tore across the yard and opened the hounds' pen. His shouts and the yammer of the hounds added to the uproar.

When Slim had put some distance behind him, the weight of the lamb dragging from his jaws slowed him to a trot. Then he heard the hounds streaking after him. Still gripping his kill, he lumbered across the prairie with the hounds gaining on him at every bound. The bell-toned yammer of their voices struck ice to his heart. He could do nothing but drop the lamb and run for his life. Still, instinct worked in him for the safety of his family. He veered away from home territory and made for Greyghost and Tawny's over on the cattle ranch.

Greyghost had been marking the eastern boundaries of his territory close to the sheep ranch, with Tawny and Silvertip tagging along for company, when the hullabaloo started.

Silvertip had had one encounter with the hounds. He

was terrified. As soon as he heard them, he streaked for the river draws, leaving Tawny and Greyghost behind. Tawny, who was almost ready to give birth, could only lumber along, hampered by a sagging bellyful of pups.

Greyghost, sensing that she was doomed if the hounds spotted her, left her to struggle on alone and waited. When Slim shot past him with the hounds hard on his heels, Greyghost dashed between, offering himself to them as an immediate target. The hounds abandoned Slim and came bellowing after him.

Greyghost could run as fast as a quarter horse for short bursts, but he was no match for hounds bred for speed. Roaring bloodlust, they strained every muscle and sinew in pursuit, gaining on him at every bound. He was headed straight for the river, but to change direction, even slightly now, was to give the hounds an advantage. With the brutes only strides behind, he had no choice but to launch himself off a cliff. He landed, five metres below, in the icy waters of the South Saskatchewan, swollen now by spring run-off.

The hounds catapulted in after him and surfaced, gagging and gasping. Their coyote-killing ardour extinguished for the moment, they floundered back to the bank and stood, shaking water off themselves and shivering. But they had no intention of going home. Not yet. They had had no exercise for a week. Dawn was breaking. The day was young. Adventure beckoned.

At the sound of the uproar, the lambing crew had tumbled out of the bunkhouse, minus shirts, their boot laces flapping about their ankles, while Jake raged, "A coyote sneaked in right by the lambing shed and snaffled a lamb!"

"Son-of-a gun! The herder *said* he figured there might be a pair of coyotes with a den down in one of the –" one of the crew began.

"The herder said?" Jake exploded. "And never told me?"

Another old guy, wise in the ways of coyotes, said, "Well, the coyote's had his taste of mutton now, Jake. He'll be back for more. Best thing you can do is phone the predator specialist from the government to come and clean the den out."

"I'm not phoning any predator specialist. Everything I need for denning coyotes is in my truck box right now," Jake said, as he slammed into the pickup and roared off toward the river draws through the strengthening dawn.

Chapter Nine

When Jake found what he knew was likely coyote denning territory, he took a long iron probe bar and a shovel from the pickup. He also snatched the rifle from its sling behind the driver's seat, but when he pulled back the bolt he found the rifle's chamber empty.

And me with a new box of ammo sitting on a shelf in the kitchen! he fumed. *Well, I'm not going back for it. Even if the mother gets away, when I find the den, I'll get the pups.*

Half an hour later he came upon a hole in the bank of a river draw, a den betrayed by small trails converging upon it. He shone his flashlight into the mouth, but he could see nothing in the curved tunnel.

Pups gotta be in there, though. The mother, too, probably.

He dropped his jacket over the den mouth, shovelled dirt over it to bar the bitch's escape, then climbed up on the bank and drove the probe bar through the earth, assessing the length and direction of the tunnel. After ten minutes of furious exertion, he was sure the bar was driving into what must be the den itself, but there was no sound, nothing to indicate that coyotes were inside. He grabbed the shovel and heaved away the overburden of earth. When he broke into the den and knelt to shine his flashlight inside, the den was empty.

Moved the pups! Well, they've got another den around here someplace.

But he slogged up and down the river banks all morning, and found nothing. He was floundering through a draw choked with saskatoon bushes and wild clematis when he heard a coyote's sharp yip. He looked up to see Slim limping along the top of the bank.

The male! Must be. Hounds missed him. Well, I'm right on top of a den or he wouldn't be hanging around yapping at me.

With the shovel in one hand and the probe bar in the other, he flailed through the tangled bush, but again he found nothing.

When he finally gave up, he did not know that Dusty was

staring at him from the mouth of a den a few feet from where he stood, terror flaring in her green eyes as she watched him wipe sweat from his brow with the arm of his shirt.

Heck with floundering around half killing myself. The hounds'll be home by now. Fetch 'em out here, then we'll see some action.

He was loading the hounds into his coyote wagon, when Dunc Ferguson drove into the yard, climbed out of his beaten-up old pickup, and stalked across to him.

"You turnin' them brutes loose again?"

"Gotta earn their keep. They missed the coyote that ran off with one of our –" He broke off, reading the old man's face. "Something wrong, Dunc?"

"Could say that. Them curs ran one of my registered Charolais cows into a barbed wire fence. Cut her up so bad I had to shoot her. Worth a cool three thousand. Due to calve in a week, too, so I lost –"

"Jeez! I'm – You're sure it was my –?"

"Caught 'em in the act. Had to go back to the house to get the rifle so I could put the cow outta her misery or I'd a been over here an hour ago. Them curs were gone by that time. Otherwise I'd a shot them, too." He advanced on Jake and tapped his chest with a horny finger.

"Get rid a them brutes. Take 'em out and shoot 'em. When you're done, get your butt over to my place. And you'd better have your cheque book in your pocket."

"But - But – Couldn't this wait till –?"

"Couldn't wait for nothing. Move it, or I go to the law. You've stomped on my toes once too often, young fella."

"But – But three thousand?!"

"Ford your drivin's a pretty nice truck. I'll take her in lieu of cash if that's the way you wanna do it."

"But the Ford's worth a lot more than –"

"So's the cow, when you figure in the calf."

Jake was feeling very hard done by when he watched Dunc drive away.

"Shoot the hounds?" he muttered. "But I can't *do* that. Long as I get rid of 'em – There was that guy down around Grassy Lake that was after 'em, too. Maybe if I phoned him..."

The guy allowed that he *would* take the hounds off Jake's hands as a kind of a favour, but when Jake told him that he had to pick them up that very afternoon, the guy became coy. Offered Jake half of what he'd paid for the hounds and refused to take them at all unless Jake threw the new canopy on the back of his pickup into the deal so that the guy could put it on his pickup to make a coyote wagon.

*T*he moment Jake had driven away to get the hounds, Slim had made for the den. Dusty emerged to greet him, hair spiked on her back. Huffing and snorting, the pair examined Jake's footprints. Then Dusty disappeared into the den and emerged, a two-and-a-half-week-old pup, grasped awkwardly by one ham, dangling from her jaws. She made off with it, heading for one of her other dens over in the next draw. Slim retrieved a second puppy and limped after her. Neither parent had eaten since the previous day; even before they started spiriting their brood to safety they were starving, and Slim was approaching the point of complete exhaustion.

As soon as they had finished moving pups, he sneaked back, looking for the lamb he had dropped the night before, but it was gone. One of the lambing crew had picked it up and taken it back for the collies at the ranch. Then, weary and footsore though he was, Slim took to the prairies. He licked up a few killdeer eggs he found beside a slough, but they didn't amount to much. Not much at all. He stared hungrily at flotillas of mallards and their ducklings out of his reach in the deep water of a slough, then he scared up a jackrabbit. But hunting alone, he had no hope of catching it. Two hours later, aside from a few voles,

a couple of garter snakes, and some sleepy grass hoppers, he had found nothing.

Apprehensive though he was, he sneaked back to the sheep ranch. His nose told him that the hounds, at least, were gone. That gave him courage. He waited until the old man with the lantern disappeared into the shed, then snaffled another lamb and fled.

When the sheep herder realized what had happened, he was wild. "The Thorne ranch has nae lost a lamb tae coyotes since I came here back in '45, and now, two in two nights?"

Young Jake couldn't meet his eye. "Guess I'd better get that coyote guy from the government out here, eh?" he ventured.

"Aye. More's the shame," the herder said, fixing Jake with a flinty and accusing eye.

So, the old coot knows I fell asleep on the job, Jake thought defiantly. *So what? They're my sheep, and as soon as lambing's done, I'm giving him the can.*

Chapter Ten

When Greyghost landed in the river, the current carried him a mile downstream before he could flounder out on the far side. As soon as he did, his nose warned him that he had landed on Squall and Limpy's territory. With their own thriving family to consider, they needed every scrap of game here for themselves. If they caught him they would show him no mercy. He dared not take time, even to rest.

The river now was in flood. When Greyghost launched himself back into the water, swirling eddies pocked its surface. Logs blundered past, snagging against hidden boulders, as did the rotting bodies of cattle. The current caught Greyghost like a wood chip and doused him in an eddy.

He fought to the surface. Panic gripped him as a log descended upon him. He struggled from its path. A hidden boulder up-ended him. He gulped water, gagged and choked, struggling to keep his nose above the surface, narrowly evading logs and tangles of debris.

After he'd dragged himself out on the far side, he lay shivering and exhausted among the fishy-smelling rocks, but his concern for Tawny would not let him rest. Since he did not know where the hounds might be, he dared not call to her in case he should attract their attention. He was creeping up the draw where he had helped her prepare her den in the old badger's diggings when Silvertip bounded out to greet him. They sniffed cautiously, nose to nose, then Greyghost made for the den with Silvertip keeping a respectful distance behind.

From the depth of the den, Tawny's low whine greeted Greyghost. Then he heard her straining grunts as she gave birth. He took one step into the tunnel, but Tawny's snarl warned him to come no farther. He would not be allowed to enter the den, nor would he be allowed to see his babies until he himself could coax them out into the sunshine.

Inside the den, Tawny leaned against the earthen wall, panting rapidly. One fuzzy baby, born twenty minutes before, climbed mewling through her fur, searching for a teat. For the moment, she ignored it as the rippling strains of a birth contraction passed through her body. A grunting heave and another puppy slipped to the floor of the den. She cleaned it and dried it while it squalled helplessly under the caress of her tongue. After she had eaten the placenta, she lay down, curled the warmth of her body around her babies and rested until the next puppy was due.

The first-born's nose, blundering blindly along her belly, bumped against a teat. In a moment, the puppy had it in its mouth. Its tail curved with pleasure, its neck arched, and it sucked enthusiastically, rolling its head from side to side, kneading its mother's belly with its forefeet. The second puppy found a teat, too, and began to nurse.

When the last of the six had been born and tended, Tawny left them briefly, emerged into the starlight, trotted away from the den, relieved herself, vomited placentas, then drank at the river's edge before she turned her attention to Greyghost.

During the past weeks, instinct had driven her to ingratiate herself with the males, since she would be dependent on them for food after the puppies were born. She had fawned on both Greyghost and Silvertip at every opportu-

nity, and the more she fawned the more responsive they had become.

Now she greeted Greyghost, licking his muzzle and urging him to regurgitate, but after his ordeal in the river his belly was empty. When he hung his head and turned away, Tawny brushed past him and hurried back to her brood.

In spite of his exhaustion, Greyghost headed out to forage. When he reached the hayfield, he discovered that Dunc had dragged an irrigation spray system out into the field that afternoon. In time, Greyghost would become used to the spray system, but he hadn't lived for more than five years by taking chances on the unknown. Weary though he was, he skirted the hayfield where Silvertip was hunting voles and headed for a slough where frogs filled the night with their croaking chorus. He caught several, but it was cold work, stalking them in the chilly water.

Then he heard the uneasy croak of a duck who was

brooding eggs in a nest hidden in the reeds at the edge of the slough. He eased out of the water and, to allay her suspicions, made a show of trotting carelessly away from the slough before he circled back and approached the nest from the far side.

With the duck and her eggs in his belly, he hurried back to the den, only to find Tawny licking Silvertip's lips, urging *him* to regurgitate. Flooded with jealous rage, he rushed Silvertip, who skedaddled, but not even Greyghost could have driven him away from the puppies. Without ever seeing them, he had fallen in love. Whenever he got a chance, he sniffed at the den opening, yawning in expectation and wiggling with pleasure at the birdlike sounds coming from within.

For the first few days after her puppies were born,

Tawny scarcely moved from them. Their body temperatures had not yet settled down; they needed their mother for warmth. They nursed until their little bellies bulged, then, after Tawny had groomed them, they crawled through her fur and fell suddenly into twitching sleep.

Greyghost and Silvertip worked overtime keeping her supplied with game. Nothing remotely edible was ignored.

Trotting along the ruts left by old Dunc's truck one rainy night, Silvertip came upon the crushed body of a rattlesnake. He eased toward the find. With his nose an inch from it, terror stabbed him. He landed eight feet away, heart thundering, hackles raised. But the snake had not moved. Surely it was dead? Silvertip snatched the body and flipped it far out into the grass, just to be sure, then he started feeding, devouring every morsel, excepting for the venomous triangle of the head and the horn-like rattles at the end of its tail.

Tawny rushed out to meet him when he returned to the den, wolfed the partially digested rattler, and returned to her brood, leaving Silvertip hungry, wet, and shivering in his half-moulted spring coat.

Since Tawny had gotten wet too, she paused in the tunnel to lick her coat partially dry before she returned to her puppies. While she was doing so, she stopped repeatedly, her attention caught by the distressed mewling of the runt which had crawled away from the warmth of its litter mates.

Tawny went to it, rolled it onto its back, groomed it, forcing it to urinate and defecate, then packed it back to the other pups who were sleeping in a tangle to share body heat. The runt rolled to its belly, head weaving blindly, but lacking the instinct to burrow into its litter mates' protective warmth, it crawled away toward the chilly earthen wall of the den.

Tawny did not retrieve it. After she had groomed the others, she stepped carefully among them and lay down. Five blunt little noses blundered eagerly along her belly, found teats, and gurgled milk while the runt mewled alone in the cold. Tawny curled around the others and ignored it. Gradually, its cries died into silence.

Four hours later, when Tawny roused to groom the others, the runt was dead. She examined it as she might have examined the body a dead bird, and when Greyghost called her to come and feed, she carried the pup out and dropped it carelessly beside the den.

Before the coyote guy arrived at Jake's sheep ranch, Slim had made off with two more lambs. His puppies, who had just started to play with each other after they'd gotten their eyes open, were doing fine.

The coyote guy made it absolutely clear that he did not want any interference from anybody on the ranch, then he went off and slogged through the river draws for two days. Toward the evening of the second, Jake looked up from the supper table to see the guy packing his rifle and his gun brace into his pickup, getting ready to pull out. Jake went out to speak to him.

"You get the coyotes?"

"Yep."

"You're sure?"

"Listen, I've got me a coyote caller that sounds so much like a dyin' rabbit that I've had hungry coyotes practically

run up my gun barrel, and them little coyotes out there were plenty hungry."

"But what about the pups?"

"Got 'em in the den with a sulphur dioxide cartridge. Eight of 'em." He shook his head. "No wonder that poor little male was so skinny. He musta been busting his ass, trying to keep his mate fed."

"Yeah! On my lambs."

"Ach, you only lost four. The place I just come from had six ewes come trailing home with their guts dragging one mornin' last week."

"Well, there you go. If I had my way, you guys would clean out every coyote in the country."

"We only take out a coyote when it starts to be a problem. Old coyote's got his place, y'know. If it wasn't for him, the voles and jackrabbits would be –"

"So Grandpa said."

"Oh, I gotta admit the coyotes are wicked on sheep once they get started, but the sheep's just about the most helpless critter God put on earth anyhow. Coyotes get the odd pronghorn or mule deer fawn, too. The weak ones, the dumb ones, and some that are just plain unlucky. But in the long run, they're doing the species a favour, leaving the best to breed."

"While every coyote's left to breed!"

"Not exactly. Last winter, when a lot of cattle died, the coyotes did okay, but next year, if there's hardly any snow and no winter-killed stock, seventy-five percent of the coyotes'll starve, or die of diseases they catch when they're not eatin' too good. Hepatitis, distemper, mange – you name it. Don't kid yourself. Life's no picnic for *canis latrans.*"

"*Canis latrans?*"

"Singin' dog, that's what it means." The guy laughed, "My grandpa had an old Mexican cowpuncher workin' for him one time. Gawd, but José loved to hear the coyotes sing. Sounded pretty much like a coyote himself when he started singin' and whangin' his old guitar."

He hopped into the pickup, slammed the door and rolled the window down. "Well, gotta get along home. Wife's expecting a baby any time now, and I wanna be around when it happens."

Chapter Eleven

*T*he puppies grew enormously during their first two weeks. Cinnamon coloured guard hairs began to cover their fuzzy greyness. When their ears and eyes first opened, sounds startled them. Sight, at first, was such a scary thing that they backed away, even from Tawny, until they felt her touch.

Differences were apparent between them right from the start. The biggest pup was an aggressive female. Bossy. She snarled and clawed her brothers and sisters out of her way to get at a teat before she even had her eyes open. Big Boy was her equal in size but not in aggression. The other three, Sly, Tawny's other male, and the two females, Sandy and Swifty, were all a bit shy, a bit on the small side.

Except for grooming and feeding them every four hours, Tawny now spent her time outside with Greyghost and Silvertip, leaving her brood to sleep, heaped together, eyelids twitching as though in dreams, and legs scrambling in tiny running motions.

Greyghost yearned to see his family. He listened at the mouth of the den at every opportunity, cocking his head from side to side and whining with longing. When the puppies were almost three weeks old, he started making coaxing sounds to lure them outside.

One morning Bossy toddled to the entrance of the den, cowered for a moment in the brilliant light, then tumbled out into the sunshine. Greyghost nosed her avidly, grinning, tail waving in wide arcs of delight.

At first, Bossy edged away from her sire, ears flattened, then she spotted Tawny and made for her. Tawny gave her one perfunctory lick before she retreated in high-stepping distaste. Bossy looked puzzled, a little uncertain, then, delighted with her new world, she attempted an awkward caper, lost her balance and blundered, nose first, into a clump of grass.

As the other puppies timidly emerged, Greyghost greeted them, each in turn, knocking them off their unsteady feet as he enthusiastically sniffed them over.

Silvertip, watching from up the bank, wiggled with a delight that he could scarcely contain as he watched. But he knew better than to intrude upon Greyghost, who had flopped to his side among his family, tongue lolling and eyes half closed with pleasure while the puppies swarmed over him. But when Bossy began searching Greyghost's belly for teats, he sprang to his feet and retreated with an expression of huffy embarrassment.

Squeaking eagerly, the pups toddled after him. Greyghost paused to sniff among them, but when Bossy and Big Boy reached for his belly again, Greyghost sprang up a bank where they couldn't follow. The pups bumbled about at the base, looking for him until the joy of freedom, in a day filled with the songs of carolling meadowlarks, sent them hopping and tumbling about like drunken bees.

When a red-tailed hawk sailed into view high above the river bank, Tawny sprang to her feet. At her low half wail the puppies scuttled into the den, collapsed in a heap in its farthest depths, and lay absolutely silent. Young though they were, Tawny did not have to warn them a second time. For two hours, she did not go near them, then, after she had nursed them and groomed them, she allowed them to follow her out into the sunshine again.

While they were distracted by Greyghost, Tawny escaped up the bank beyond their reach, moving to a vantage point, downwind, where she could keep an eye on both her brood and her surroundings. Greyghost, too, climbed to a spot where the puppies could not follow, yawned, stretched out in the sun, and closed his eyes.

Silvertip's turn. At last! He slipped down the bank, joyfully sniffed the puppies over, knocked them off their feet, flattened them each in turn, groomed them until they squeaked and wriggled in protest, and finally collapsed among them, wearing an expression of daffy adoration.

Thus began the summer of his subjugation. For almost six months he would feed the pups, guard them, groom them, play with them, teach them to sing, suffer their attacks on his tail and on his ears, and suffer Greyghost's scant tolerance of his presence until the youngsters were grown and gone.

*I*n comparison to Silvertip's experience, Shadow's, at least in the beginning, was nothing short of idyllic. After their initial hostile challenge, Squall and Limpy took her to their bosoms. The three lazed about together and greeted each other affectionately after any parting. For a long time, no human crossed the abandoned farm where they lived, game there was sufficient to their needs, and since Shadow and Squall were both tireless hunters, feeding Limpy after her three puppies were born was no trouble at all.

Chapter Twelve

Distances shimmered in an early June heat wave, the prairie wool curled and turned brown, and the prickly pear cacti opened their huge rose and yellow flowers to the sun.

Greyghost and Tawny, along with Silvertip, too hot to move more than necessary, were flopped out, panting in the heat, keeping one eye on their surroundings and the other on the three-week-old puppies. Even the pups were lethargic, but they still engaged in the curious rituals common to all young coyotes. A pair would circle, sometimes for minutes at time, each with its chin resting on the other's rump. The ritual seemed to have no reason, to offer no pleasure, but the pups engaged in it many times a day, turning around and around each other, as solemn as undertakers.

There was another ritual, too. Dominant pups would stand with their forefeet planted on the shoulders of lesser beings. Although the weaker pups objected to being used in such a manner, they could do nothing but submit to the indignity.

There were lots of fun games, too. In spite of the heat, Swifty, Sandy, and Sly had started a little game of "I'll bump you and you chase me," when Tawny spotted a man at the head of the draw who was amusing himself by wandering about shooting gophers. He never saw the coyotes, but the moment the coyotes saw him, Tawny sent the pups scuttling into the den. Then she and the other adults flattened to earth and bellied out of the draw.

The man never came close to the den, but in Tawny's eyes, the site had been violated. The moment the man left, she returned, snatched Big Boy, and made off with him, headed for one of the other dens that she had prepared. Greyghost followed with Bossy squirming in his jaws, banging her head on the ground at every step as he trotted off with her.

Silvertip was left to guard Sly and the two little females.

That was easy; Tawny had given them such a fright that they never moved, let alone came near the den mouth.

When Tawny returned for the last pup, Silvertip trailed her to the new den. There he was left to guard the puppies again while Tawny and Greyghost made separate trips back to the old quarters, checking to make sure no puppy had been left behind. The pups, sternly warned, cuddled silently together, all rivalries for the moment forgotten.

Although moving them had been a difficult task, there were advantages in the new quarters; thousands of ticks and fleas had been left behind, and the new territory provided a fresh supply of voles.

The disadvantage the coyotes had not foreseen. That spring, after Tawny had prepared her spare dens, a pair of great horned owls, who like nothing so much as coyote meat, had built a nest in a Balm o' Gilead beside the river not far from the den where the coyotes had moved the puppies. They had not seen the owls who roosted in the tree during daylight hours, very silent and very still, in case a hawk or a roving band of crows should spot them.

At dusk, when Greyghost and Silvertip went off to hunt, the owls launched themselves on silent wings and went off to hunt as well.

Tawny, who was weary and overstrung from the move, stayed behind to guard the den. As the dark came down, she began to relax. When the puppies timidly appeared at the den mouth, she did not warn them back inside. One by one, they emerged into the warm dusk and rushed about, eagerly exploring the new terrain.

At nursing time, when Tawny hopped down from her perch, where she had been resting beyond the puppies' reach, they descended on her to suck gluttonously while she stood, straddle- legged, bearing their onslaught with an expression of pained resignation. Nursing had become an ordeal; the hair on her belly was plucked bare.

Bossy, who had sprouted two needle-sharp teeth, nipped Tawny in her eagerness. Tawny whipped around, scattering pups, and nipped Bossy hard enough to hurt. Bossy yelped and scuttled away, but the other pups came staggering after Tawny, determined to continue their feast. She gaped at them threateningly. Suddenly embarrassed and unsure of her, they pretended to examine buffalo beans and sage bushes that were close at hand.

While Tawny went to Bossy and gave her a rough lick or two to indicate that she had been forgiven, Swifty discovered that she could scramble up onto a small rise of

ground. Delighted with her vantage point above her family, she barked and gave one playful hop.

That hop was her last. The owl swooped in. Before Swifty had time even to squeak, she was sailing away, squirming in the owl's clutches.

Tawny sent the other pups streaking into the den, then tore after the owl, springing into the air beneath it again and again. When it disappeared against the darkening night sky, she stopped, staring after it, and gave one doleful wail. Silvertip and Greyghost came running.

A major crisis. The puppies must be moved. Immediately. But where? The other dens Tawny had prepared were well within the owls' range.

Greyghost and Tawny had always avoided the sheep ranch, but since Slim and Dusty's demise, the ranch was free territory for any coyote's taking. It lay beyond the owls' range, and the sheep, at this time of year, were being grazed three miles away on the far side of the property.

Late that night, as Tawny explored the ranch, she came upon a perfect denning site, a shallow draw where a spring bubbled up through the rocks. Its overflow had encouraged a growth of saskatoons, chokecherries, and scrub poplars: perfect cover for pups. A huge rock, hidden by bush, protruded from halfway up the bank. Beneath its shelter she could make an ideal den.

She had dug a tunnel three feet into the earth before her teats, filled and throbbing with milk, forced her to return to her pups. After she had suckled them, she and Greyghost returned to finish the den, leaving Silvertip to watch the pups.

For more than three hours they remained in the den,

silent and uncomplaining. Then Bossy and Big Boy came to the entrance. As soon as they spotted Silvertip they capered toward him. Good old Silvertip always let them get away with murder. When he sprang to his feet, headed them off, and chased them back into the den, they looked amazed.

After sitting just inside the entrance and thinking it over, they seemed to come to the conclusion that Sivertip must have been kidding. Assuming their most appealing expressions, they made for him again. He rushed them, this time with a gaping threat.

They scampered into the den, but not into its farthest depths as they would have done at Tawny's command. They stayed at the entrance, falling into entreating poses, begging to be allowed outside. The moment Silvertip was distracted, they escaped. All afternoon he herded them back to safety. By the time Tawny and Greyghost returned at dusk, he was exhausted. So indeed were they, but still another night of hauling pups lay ahead.

Chapter Thirteen

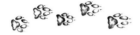

But the new den was perfect. Before the pups were four weeks old they were tearing through the safe cover of the bush, tussling with each other and playing games of nip and flee.

Greyghost introduced them to solid food, regurgitating for them one morning when he returned from hunting. At first, they merely messed in the food, but when Tawny nipped in and started eating it from under their noses, they began choking it down before she could do so.

They played rough. They did not yet know what would hurt and what would not. Frequently they made each other cry out while they were tussling. Their grudges culminated in a major fight, which broke out one morning when they were four weeks old. The row started over a bit of sage branch that Silvertip had brought home for them to play with.

Sandy got the branch first. Big Boy snatched it from her. Sly and he were playing tug-of-war for possession of it when Sandy's outrage boiled over. She piled into both of them. Bossy, who never could mind her own business, got into the act. For fifteen seconds the pups were a tiny whirlwind of shrieks and needle-toothed aggression, but that fifteen seconds settled for all time Sly and Sandy's lowly position in the hierarchy.

Big Boy and Bossy still had a round to go. That afternoon, the bit of sage forgotten, the two were intent on a game of chasing their own tails when they collided. Big Boy took offence, sank his teeth into Bossy's neck, and shook her until she cried for mercy. But Bossy was not to be vanquished.

When Silvertip showed up, carrying a dead mouse, she sprang at his face, snatched the mouse and started a game of her own, chewing the mouse, tossing it away, pouncing on it again, and daring Big Boy to touch it.

Sandy and Sly wanted the mouse too, but they knew better than to challenge Bossy. For a while they watched wistfully, then, as they were going off to torment Silvertip, Big

Boy nipped in, snatched the mouse, and took off with it.

Bossy squealed with outrage and chased him through the bush, up the bank and down the bank and through the spring, around and around until Big Boy eluded her, got beyond her sight, tumbled into a small gully, and lay perfectly still. Bossy dropped to her haunches, ears pricked, listening.

When she heard Big Boy begin his own game of fling and pounce, she bellied forward, waited until his back was turned, launched herself from the rim of the gully, sank her teeth into his rump just above his tail, where he could not get at her to retaliate, and held on. He shrieked and flung himself this way and that, but he could not break her hold.

Looking a trifle alarmed, Greyghost came to his rescue. He grabbed Bossy by one ham, dragged her away, held her down, and tried to groom her. She squirmed away from him and made for Big Boy again. Big Boy abandoned the mouse and fled.

Now top dog, and triumphant, Bossy took the mouse back to flaunt under the noses of the other pups. None challenged her, but her victory had its price; now everybody mistrusted her. Afterwards, when the others ripped through the bush in games of tag, or took each other down in mock wrestles, Bossy had to beg her way into the game or they would not play with her.

Silvertip adored the pups, allowed them liberties their parents would never have tolerated, and worked overtime hunting voles to feed them. One morning, just as it was getting light, he was trotting through Wally Johnson's pasture on his way back to the den with a nice bellyful of voles for the pups when he stumbled across a hen that was brooding a clutch of eggs in a nest she'd made for herself out in the pasture.

What Silvertip did not know while he was trotting triumphantly away with the hen in his mouth, was that Wally was sitting in front of the picture window in the house, smoking a cigarette, and watching the dawn come up. He was deeply angry, deeply disturbed. In less than a month, he and his wife would have no choice but to move off the place and abandon it to the bank which held the mortgage. For weeks he had not been able to sleep.

"Coyote!" he growled when he spotted Silvertip. "That's the little grey sucker that was getting fat on our stock last winter. Well, that's it. We're not running a buffet for him no more."

He went to a gun cabinet and unlocked it. "Gonna lay for him. Gonna leave the hen house door open and offer him more bait. One of these mornings I'm gonna blow him clean to kingdom come."

Chapter Fourteen

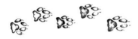

As the days went on, the pups' coats lightened in colour, their ears grew larger, and their snouts lengthened into real coyote faces. Life was a great adventure. All day long they ambushed brothers and sisters in games of "hide and pounce" or chased each other in the game of "I'll bump you and you chase me." Often the baby-sitters engaged the pups in wild games of tag. Occasionally the sires joined in, but Tawny and Limpy remained aloof. They still suffered the pups' playful attacks on their tails and their ears and they continued to nurse them, although all the pups had sprouted teeth.

Limpy and Squall's puppies were a few days short of five weeks old when their idyllic life came to an abrupt end. One day a coyote wagon pulled onto their abandoned farm. It was the guy from down around Grassy Lake who had bought Jake Thorne's hounds.

As he bumped across the old farm, he spotted Squall trotting along with a young gopher in his mouth. Immediately the guy turned the hounds loose. Squall didn't stand a chance. The hounds ripped both him and the gopher apart.

The moment the coyote wagon had appeared, Limpy dived into the den with the pups and kept absolutely still. Shadow took to the prairie. She didn't return to the den until almost dark. By that time, the guy and his hounds had been gone a long time and Limpy was struggling to move the second of her three pups to the safety of another den.

In order to pack five-week-old pups she had had to use her crippled foot. Her injury from the trap last winter had been severe. The foot had only superficially healed. Before the second move was completed, a bone had broken through the old scab. The injury became infected.

In a day or so, Limpy was in serious trouble and her milk dried up. The puppies were ravenous. Even while Limpy was dying and past the point of being able to ward them off, they tried to suckle, while Shadow coaxed them to try the regurgitated meat that she supplied.

*T*he day that Tawny's pups were five weeks old, she weaned them. Chop. Just like that. That morning, when she returned from hunting, the pups descended on her, falling over each other in their eagerness. She evaded them, and for the first time, regurgitated food for them.

They wanted milk. They evaded what she had supplied and made for their mother. She trotted away in high-stepping irritation. The pups galloped after her. She whipped around with a threatening gape. They skidded to a stop, regarding her with dismayed expressions before retreating to gulp down the food that she had supplied. But they were not satisfied. They wanted milk.

One by one, they bellied toward her, tails pumping and mouths working in entreaty and greedy desire. She rushed them and scattered them. They hid behind stones and bushes and peeped out at her. Her shrewish expression was warning enough for Sly and Sandy, but Bossy and Big Boy weren't so easily fazed.

The moment Tawny started to relax, they crept toward her again. She bowled Big Boy over and nipped him until he cried for mercy, then she went after Bossy. Even Sandy and Sly came in for a trouncing when she was done with Bossy.

The pups finally hid from her, but they did not have the

self-discipline to stay hidden for long. Whenever one forgot and showed itself, Tawny was upon it. Finally, they all retreated deep into the bush.

When Silvertip, all unaware, arrived home with a bellyful of chicken and a coppery red chicken's wing for the pups to play with, they were nowhere to be seen. He called to them anxiously. They answered from their hiding places, but they would not show themselves. Silvertip went to round them up. They tumbled toward him, pathetically relieved to see him, and so puzzled by the day's turn of events that they didn't even quarrel over the chicken wing that he'd brought for them.

After he'd fed them, Silvertip led them off, circling wide from the den where Tawny waited, and headed for the spring. The pups had often played messy games in the water, but, aside from the odd experimental lap, they had never drunk from it. Now they were thirsty and hot after hours of hiding in the bush. They lapped eagerly from the spring's overflow.

All that afternoon a cobalt cloud built in the western sky. When brilliant forks of lightning started sizzling in its depths and thunder began to growl, the puppies huddled nervously around Silvertip. Greyghost appeared when the first cuff of wind rocked the sage and flattened the grass.

While Silvertip trotted away as though he had business elsewhere, Greyghost led the puppies back to the den. Tawny, who had been lying at the entrance, got up and moved away. Without so much as a glance at their mother, the pups disappeared into the tunnel as an onslaught of rain drenched the earth.

For the first time since the puppies were born, Tawny stayed out in the rain with the males. When the thunderstorm rolled away and a rainbow arched from horizon to horizon across the eastern sky, the adult coyotes started a wild romp to warm themselves, while the puppies eased outside, watching with wistful expressions. When Tawny approached, they dived for shelter. As the sun disappeared, she scrambled to the top of the muddy bank and lifted her voice in what could only be called a yodel of celebration for freedom won.

The pups were uncertain of Tawny after that. Although she always regurgitated food for them when she returned from hunting, she often engaged them in roughhouse antics that were more punishment than play.

*T*he same night that Tawny was celebrating her freedom, Shadow found herself shackled with three ram-
bunctious responsibilities – Squall and Limpy's puppies.

At first they seemed to think that she was only the
babysitter. Her say didn't count. For two days she trailed
anxiously behind them, trying to keep them out of danger,
but the morning she heard the guy from down around
Grassy Lake approaching in his coyote wagon, she
trounced the puppies, one after the other, and sent them
scuttling into the den with the threat of plenty more where
that came from, before she took to the prairie herself.

All day she did not go near the puppies. The following
morning before dawn, when she returned and called them
out to feed, there was no longer any question who was
boss, but it would be many weeks before the puppies could
hunt for themselves. All that summer Shadow ran herself
skinny and footsore keeping them fed.

When the pups' instinct to hunt for themselves finally
began to assert itself, they began stalking grasshoppers.
Before long they could hold a point with perfect concentration. When their spring-and-pounce efforts were successful,
they discovered that grasshoppers were pretty good eating.

But they were still very much puppies. There were

always games after they grew tired of hunting, although the solitary instinct was beginning to assert itself. Often one or another found a spot beside some sage bush, away from the rest of the family, curled into a ball, and fell asleep.

Soon Shadow began bringing home live voles in her belly to teach them hunting skills. Not only had the unfortunate voles been swallowed alive before being coughed up for the pups, but as soon as it seemed that they might have a chance to escape, a pup would pounce on them, flip them into the air, allow them to escape, then pounce on them again. Finally, when a vole was too stunned and slow to be any fun, the pup would shake it to death and eat it.

*N*ot wanting to draw attention to themselves while the pups were very young, Tawny and Greyghost had sung only under cover of darkness, but now they resumed their joyous morning and evening yip-howl sessions with the pups joining in. Little by little, under Silvertip's instruction, the youngsters' high-pitched squawks and wails began to sound like real coyote songs. Often they heard Shadow's crew from across the river. She had taught hers to sing very well too, a most necessary accomplishment for any self-respecting coyote.

At six weeks, all the pups were bundles of energy, bundles of curiosity. Nothing fazed them. Whatever they blundered across must be bitten, chased, tasted or tormented. The adults never returned to the den without coughing up a mouse so that the pups could squabble over that and leave them in peace.

Then, suddenly, at eight weeks, everything changed; the most familiar objects became threats, became dangers. After giving the pups weeks of unbridled freedom in a seemingly unthreatening world, nature put on the brakes. Caution awakened. Fear awakened. The distant scream of a hawk flattened them to the earth.

Shadow bringing home an eagle quill that she'd found for her tribe to play with, was enough to fill them with terror. An old stick that Silvertip's charges had chewed on happily the previous day, they viewed with extreme suspicion the next. His tearing through the bush with the lower jaw of a pronghorn's skull, the pups' favourite plaything, sent them scuttling for cover.

Chapter Fifteen

Silvertip had gotten away with five of Wally Johnson's chickens, and Wally was still vowing to "blast that coyote clean to kingdom come," but every morning, while he sat in the open doorway, rifle at the ready, waiting for Silvertip to appear, he dropped off. One morning, the distant crowing of a rooster jerked him awake. He couldn't see the rooster, but he could hear it.

So could Silvertip, who had been hiding in the long brome grass at the edge of the pasture, waiting for the chickens to appear. What neither he nor Wally knew was that a gust of wind during the night had slammed the hen house door and the chickens couldn't get out.

Tired of waiting, Silvertip decided to explore the farmyard to see if there was anything else he might scare up. He had never before taken such a chance, but he'd become a little overconfident. A little careless.

Fortunately for him, he did at least circle wide of the house. He was trotting past the back of the barn where the coyote traps hung when he caught the faintest whiff of his own dried-up toe in one of the trap's teeth.

As he streaked away, Wally's rifle cracked. A bullet zinged past, so close to Silvertip that it stirred the ruff of fur around his face. His heart was still pounding when he got back to the den and engaged the puppies in a rowdy game of tag to calm his nerves.

*B*y the time the pups were nine weeks old, they had all outgrown their week of timidity. Now they were merely cautious about things they had not seen before or things they did not understand.

Tawny, taking her brood's education upon herself, decided that the time had come when they needed a lesson in self-reliance. One morning she led them down through the bush, parked them at a den in the middle of some long rye grass out on the open plain, and threatened them with

a trouncing when they tried to follow her back. As soon as she left, they dived into the strange den and crowded together in a nervous huddle, but after a while Bossy and Big Boy became curious enough to venture out. Sandy and Sly timidly joined them.

For a while they all huddled together, staring about, bewildered and lost. Then Big Boy discovered a dung beetle that he could torment. Bossy began stalking a sleepy grasshopper on a stem of rye grass, and Sandy spotted something that she knew must be a vole moving in the grass. She rose stealthily and gathered herself, eyes fixed, never allowing her concentration to waver from the tiny shifting at the grass roots. Certain of the vole's position finally, she jack-knifed, landed, and snatched the stunned prize.

Instantly, Bossy and Big Boy were upon her. She ducked away. Big Boy cut her off. She swung to avoid him, smacked into Sly, and dropped the vole. It scuttled for cover and escaped, but now they *knew!* They were still trying to catch voles when Tawny rounded them up to take them back to Home Place at sunset.

Before many days had passed, they had learned to find their way between Home Place and the den where Tawny parked them, and they had all learned to catch voles. Bossy even caught a baby gopher.

By the end of July they were adolescents, starving, rowdy, and swift as light. The dens were abandoned. Both Tawny and Shadow began parking their charges in willow scrub or buck brush thickets on either side of the river, where they would be safe during the day, each in its own small territory, and where they could practice hunting skills.

When night came, they rounded their charges up and took them on hunting expeditions. During their first nighttime forays, the pups clung to the adults, ears back and tails down, but once they'd caught a vole or two, their confidence grew. Soon hunting out in the dark became a great adventure.

The year now was at high summer, the vole population abundant. The prairie twilights were redolent with dusty sage, warmed from the day-long sun, the nights adrift with silent thunderheads, their hearts flaming intermittently with rose-gold lightning.

· By the end of August all the pups were almost fully grown. They worked hard at trying to feed themselves, but until they had their full set of second teeth they were still depending on the food that the adults supplied when they visited each in its hiding place before dawn.

Like all pups, they had an irresistible urge to chew, since they needed to dislodge their baby teeth. Once, on a day in late August, Bossy left her patch of willow scrub to find a horse bone that she had seen up on the river bank. As she gnawed, a molar in the back of her mouth bent and dislodged. Erupting beneath was a jagged instrument designed for tearing meat. In another month she would have the tools of a very efficient hunter.

But, as it happened, she spotted a rattlesnake making its way down the bank toward its hibernation den. At her approach, the snake drew itself into a defensive coil. The tip of its tail buzzed a warning.

Bossy was intrigued. She had never seen a rattlesnake. Garter snakes always slithered away, trying to escape whenever she went after them, but this creature coiled tighter,

raising half the length of its body from its coil. Wherever Bossy moved, the snake's head followed and the buzz of its tail intensified.

But Bossy knew it was meat. Tempting. And as usual, she was hungry. Still keeping her distance, she scuffed her nose provocatively through the dust and flirted to one side. The snake's head turned to follow. Bossy danced forward and made a lightning feint.

The snake struck. Its fangs snagged in the earth. The creature snapped back into its coil, buzzing furiously.

Bossy tossed her head and circled at a saucy prance. She dashed in twice, both times evading the snake's strike, then gathering herself for her next dash, she sidled in close.

The snake struck again. That time its fangs lodged in the end of her nose. She yelped and shuddered away. The snake disengaged its fangs, recoiled itself, and stared at her through the slitted irises of its unblinking eyes.

Bossy staggered away, looking bewildered. Minutes later, as the powerful venom coursed through her bloodstream, she collapsed in a shuddering heap.

The snake nosed her, realized that she was too big for him to swallow, then undulated on down the bank, his flicking tongue listening for him, and his rattles clicking softly.

Chapter Sixteen

At the end of September the prairie lay in quiet shades of washed-out golds, umbers, and greys, and the winds, for once, were still. Sometimes, in the early morning, ghostly mirages rose above the horizon, trembled there for a minute or two, then distorted, wavered, and disappeared.

Already there had been hard frosts, and with the colder nights, the coyotes' coats lengthened and thickened. The pups now were fully grown. The adults would no longer tolerate them on hunting expeditions. Frequently the male pups disappeared on small forays, testing their readiness to strike out on their own, but they still returned before dawn. Sandy stayed within hollering distance of Greyghost and Tawny, hiding in this patch of rose briers or that patch of buck brush, and managing to catch enough voles to satisfy her needs.

Silvertip's bond with the family was disintegrating. Tawny was no longer chummy with him; Greyghost and he avoided each other. Silvertip became surly with the pups. He would no longer feed them, and, given the opportunity, he would steal voles from them. As soon as Greyghost quitted marking territory, the family disintegrated.

Big Boy and Sly went their separate ways. Within an hour, Tawny and Greyghost followed, with Sandy, who would become their next year's baby-sitter, tagging along.

Silvertip was left alone.

On the far side of the river, so was Shadow. The last of her orphans had struck out on their own. She was indifferent to their going. In spite of her sacrifices for the puppies, she had become as impatient with them as Silvertip had been with Greyghost and Tawny's before their departure.

That stone cold afternoon, Silvertip went to the river and stared longingly at the place where he'd last seen Shadow. Crossing was impossible now; jagged ice frilled the river's margins and sludgy near-ice moved in its current. As he turned away, a blast of Arctic air drove snow into his face. Winter was coming in, early and hard. That night, the temperature plummeted. Before morning, the river was frozen solid, bank to bank.

Silvertip was testing his footing and easing out onto the ice, heading for where he'd last seen Shadow when he heard a "wow-oo-wow" of greeting. He whipped around. There she was, standing half way up the bank, looking down at him.

They bounded toward each other, sniffing nose to nose while Shadow joyfully whipped herself with her tail. Then she sprang into the air and raced away, Silvertip on her heels. They flew over rocks, ducked around the bare Balm o' Gilead where the great horned owls had nested, tore through thickets of saskatoon and chokecherry, raced out onto the open prairie and flopped, rolling in the new snow and eyeing each other like a couple of love-drunk teenagers.

When Silvertip rose, Shadow scrunched before him, puppy fashion, before she too rose, licked his muzzle, and tapped him smartly on the nose. He examined her with a lordly dignity, then they both lifted their noses and sang to the new day.

*F*or three months they hunted voles and jackrabbits and exulted in each other's company.

Young Jake Thorne, who had finally found the nerve to fire his old sheepherder, often heard them, but he never saw them, much as he wanted to. Now he figured he had the answer to the coyote problem – a snowmobile.

"Great for either herdin' sheep or chasin' coyotes," the dealer had told him. "And this baby don't need no dog chow. Haw! Haw! Haw!"

Excepting for the one blast in late October, up until the end of January there had been scarcely enough snow for Jake to try out his new toy properly. Then a blizzard howled out of the Arctic and piled the prairie with sixty-five centimetres of snow in a single night. The next day, a capricious chinook melted the top four centimetres, but the relentless Arctic outbreak was not to be denied. It drove the chinook back across the Rockies. The melted top layer froze solid, leaving the prairies capped in ice.

A disaster for the coyotes. Voles, safe beneath the ice cover, escaped before they could break through to them. Jackrabbits skimmed across the crust that sometimes supported the coyotes, and, as often, treacherously collapsed. Within a week they were on the verge of starvation and freezing in the unrelenting cold.

Shadow, out of pure desperation, had taken to watching the sheep and allowing herself to be tempted. One day, while Jake was hauling feed to his ewes, he spotted her. As soon as he had dumped his load, he took after her, the snowmobile skimming lightly over the crust while Shadow broke through, floundered out again and again, straining every nerve and sinew trying to outrun the roaring monster at her heels.

In no time she was exhausted, breath coming in great open-mouthed gasps and heart threatening to burst. Twice Jake ran right over top of her in the deep snow, laughing his head off when he saw the dazed expression on her face.

But when Shadow unexpectedly changed direction, Jake brought the machine around in a tight turn. The skis caught in the edge of a pyramid of rock that old Bill Tardif had piled there seventy-five years before when he had been clearing the land for his homestead. The snowmobile came to a jolting stop. One ski splintered. The engine stalled. Jake sailed over the machine, and landed among the rocks. The wind was knocked out of him, and blood poured into his eyes from a cut on his forehead. A sickening jolt of pain hit him when he sat up and tried fumble his way out of the rock pile. One arm was all but useless.

"Busted collar bone. I know it," he gasped. "Well, it could have been worse. Could have been a leg. At least, I can make it over to Dunc's and ask for help."

The snow was deep, the crust treacherous, and Jake was shivering violently. "Oh, Jeez," he groaned, as he started out. "Bloody snowmobiles. Bloody sheep. Bloody coyotes."

While Shadow had been hungrily gazing at the sheep that afternoon, Silvertip was a mile away, inching across a patch of ice-covered buck brush. He heard a rustling scuttle beneath his feet. Something bigger than a vole. He froze until he had pinpointed the sound. When he broke through the snow crust, he discovered a Hungarian partridge trapped beneath the ice. After he had dispatched the one, he discovered several more.

He was emerging from the snow, gorged with partridge, intent upon finding Shadow so that he could share with her, when he heard the snowmobile. That scared him. Several times he had seen Jake ripping around on the thing, and from Jake's scent, Silvertip knew that this was the same man who had turned the hounds loose last spring. From the sounds of his whoops and hollers now, he was chasing something again.

After he heard the snowmobile stop, and Jake swearing as he walked away, Silvertip called anxiously to Shadow. She did not answer.

As soon as Silvertip was sure that Jake had gone, he started to look for her, but he could not find her. The confusing traces of her scent were contaminated by the snowmobile. He called her again and again, but she did not answer.

When he finally tracked her down, she was curled in the snow, not even shivering, deep in shock, hovering on the verge of death. The stress of being run to complete exhaustion had depleted her meager reserves.

Silvertip whined and prodded her repeatedly with his nose. For a long time she did not respond, then she winced deep within herself and stirred a little. Silvertip circled, whining and pawing at her insistently. She whimpered, lifted her head, and licked his muzzle. Immediately, he regurgitated for her.

She began to feed, violent shivering overtaking her as the food warmed her. When she wavered to her feet,

Silvertip headed for the shelter of the river draws, pausing again and again to wait for her. As she struggled to follow, step by uncertain step, the first gentle breath of a chinook from beyond the Rockies that would melt the prairie's ice cap winnowed their coats.

Tomorrow they would be hunting voles, and at moonrise they would be singing with ventriloquist's magic across the prairie distances to others of their kind.

Acknowledgements

*M*y thanks to Alberta Culture for financial help. Thanks to the Predator Division of Alberta's Department of Agriculture for inviting me along on a conference and answering my questions. Thanks to Rick Smith for inspiring me to "take another look," to Kevin Roberts for his help and encouragement, and to David Carpenter and Geoffrey Ursell for their wise counsel and careful editing.

About the Author

*B*etty Wilson is the author of two other books, including *The Book of Sarah,* published by Coteau Books in 1998, and the award-winning *André Tom MacGregor.* As well, she has published poetry and prose in numerous periodicals and anthologies. Born in Lethbridge, she grew up in Grassy Lake, Alberta, and taught school in many Alberta communities before settling in Edmonton in 1949. She retired to her current home of Nanaimo, British Columbia, in 1987.